RED RIVER RIOT

There was no doubt that Wes Santee was a drifter, so when he jumped off the freight train at the Red River town the local law was there to greet him. There was just one place for drifters! Jailed while Sheriff Kirby checked on his past, Santee came up against Will Handy and from there on it was downhill all the way for Santee: he was beaten up, ambushed and even held for murder. Finally Santee said 'To hell with it'. Now he would flush them out with guns blazing, no quarter asked and none given.

RED RIVER RIOT

RED RIVER RIOT

by

Clayton Nash

Dales Large Print Books
Long Preston, North Yorkshire,
BD23 4ND, England.

British Library Cataloguing in Publication Data.

Nash, Clayton
    Red River riot.

    A catalogue record of this book is
    available from the British Library

    ISBN   1-84262-193-9 pbk

First published in Great Britain in 2002 by Robert Hale Limited

Copyright © Clayton Nash 2002

Cover illustration © Ballestar by arrangement with
Norma Editorial S.A.

Published in Large Print 2002 by arrangement with
Robert Hale Limited

Dales Large Print is an imprint of Library Magna Books Ltd.

Printed and bound in Great Britain by
T.J. (International) Ltd., Cornwall, PL28 8RW

1
Drifter

He arrived in the Red River town of Beaumont Flats with holes in his clothes, scuffed-over boots and stony-broke. He didn't even own a gun – which was just as well in one way, because he liked guns, always had, even when they had made him more trouble than he could shake a stick at. He rode in on a seven-car freight on the Missouri, Kansas and Texas line – 'The Katy' as it was known – which had been the first railroad to enter Texas from the north and had been serving this area since 1872. The only reason he knew this was because he had found a dirty, dog-eared brochure lying amongst the straw on the floor of the boxcar he had ridden in. Not that he cared – just so long as it got him out of Fort Worth.

He slid the door part-way open, feeling the hot wind on his gaunt, stubbled face, jammed his hat down a little lower on his forehead and looked for some track-side brush to cushion his fall when he jumped. It came up as the locomotive wheezed and panted on the slow entry to the siding. He had left it a little late, he figured, and he shouldered the heavy door along the slide, picked out his clump of chaparral and leapt.

He only had a slim, battered warbag, was unencumbered by saddle or grubsacks. The dry brush crackled and splintered as his lean body hit and he rolled, experience making him instinctively cover his eyes with a hand until he was clear of the brush. He landed face down and lifted his head, spitting out the mouthful of sand, as the rest of the freight cars rumbled past. He scrabbled around quickly and couched behind the brush as the caboose approached, hunkering down so the guard couldn't see him.

The end of the train creaked and squeaked by his hiding place and slid to a stop at the siding a hundred yards down the track. He stood slowly, dusting himself down, tugging off his faded neckerchief and mopping his face. He hefted the lean-looking warbag and wondered which was the best way to enter the town that shimmered in the hot north Texas sun.

It beckoned him but he felt little enthusiasm. The towns he had picked lately seemed to having nothing to offer him except trouble. And he couldn't afford any more of that. So maybe he'd wait around out here until the sun went down – wouldn't be more than a couple of hours – and then drift in with the dusk. He liked to have a place to sleep all picked out by sundown usually, but he had heard the sheriff here was a hard son of a bitch and the longer he put off an open confrontation the better it seemed to him.

'Guess you must've lost your ticket, leavin' the train early like this.'

He whirled at the tough-sounding voice behind him, almost overbalancing, the warbag swinging. Maybe the man who had spoken thought he was going to throw it at him, for he stepped nimbly to one side and a cocked sixgun appeared in his right hand.

'Don't!'

The ragged man let the warbag fall and it crumpled in on itself, showing how empty it was. The lawman narrowed his eyes, looking over the other as he lifted his hands shoulder-high.

'Where's your gun?'

'Sold it long ago.'

'Uh-huh. Well, I don't allow broke drifters

in my town, mister. You better show me you got enough change in your pockets to buy a meal and a bed for tonight.'

'Or...?'

The cool green eyes narrowed a little more in the leathery face. 'Or I might decide to throw you in my jail for a day or two until I'm ready to kick you out.'

The man nodded. 'I heard about you – Sheriff Kirby?'

'*Abe* Kirby. And you'd be...?'

The drifter hesitated. 'Wes Santee.'

The sheriff stared and Santee could see the focus of his thoughts was a long way from this clump of chaparral. 'Sounds familiar. Where you reckon I would've heard it? Or read it?'

Santee said nothing, but he regarded this lawman warily. A man in his forties, he figured, heavy-boned, the stained frontier moustache masking his mouth almost entirely, the nose big and hooked, the stance easy and confident. The hands were big-knuckled and gnarled and there were a few scars around the eyes when Santee shifted his gaze back there. Here was a sheriff who didn't mind mixing it with men who didn't obey his orders.

'You mind putting up that gun, Sheriff?'

Santee said edgily and Kirby arched his brows.

'Makin' you nervous?'

'I've been on the wrong end of too many guns for a long time now, Sheriff. I don't want any trouble. I want work if I can get it.'

'And if you can't?'

Santee shrugged. 'I'll ride the next freight out.'

'That you won't do,' Kirby told him flatly. 'Seems to me I've seen your name on a Wanted dodger. You have any comment on that?'

'None at all.'

The sheriff's mouth lifted slightly at one corner. 'Figured not. You look like you been around. How come guns make you nervous?'

'They don't. Just tired of people pointin' 'em at me.'

'And why would they do that? Usually a man gets a gun pointed at him, he's in some kinda trouble.'

Santee sighed. 'I've had my share. Drifting. Drunk. Brawling. Broke enough to steal a pie off a windowsill. Nothing too serious.'

'Yeah, well, that's your version. I'd just better check you out, mister.' The gun-barrel jerked towards the heat-shimmering

11

buildings of town. 'Let's make you comfortable in a nice cool cell.'

Santee sighed, shaking his head slowly as he shouldered his warbag. Kirby reached out and felt the bulges carefully, sixgun still cocked and covering the drifter.

'You travel light.'

'Belly's even lighter.'

They were walking down past the siding now and the railroad workers paused briefly to watch; it wasn't usual for Sheriff Abe Kirby to hold a cocked sixgun on drifters he picked up jumping out of freight cars. They saw the way the lanky Santee moved, could tell he was hard-muscled despite his leanness, and the set of those wide shoulders made them think here was a proud man – down on his luck and hanging out of his trousers seat, maybe, but a man with pride.

They wondered if Kirby had seen the same thing? For the sheriff was a man who liked to break a man who gave him any trouble.

The cell was cool and surprisingly clean and Santee gladly stretched out on the narrow bunk. He was surprised when twenty minutes after locking him in, Kirby sent a deputy with cold pie and a cup of coffee and an apple. He wolfed down the food and it was dark before the sheriff appeared in the passage outside the cells, hanging an oil-lamp on a nail on the wall. He held two dog-eared dodgers and waved them against the bars.

'Couple years old, but it's you all right, Santee. Mixed up in a stage hold-up.'

'Hell, I've done my time for that – I only held the getaway mounts. They gave me six months in Yuma.'

'So you says. You're gonna have to stick around till I check it out. Take two, three days, mebbe a little longer.'

'Well, I can stand it if you can. Thanks for the grub, Kirby. At least I'll have somewhere to sleep.'

The sheriff grunted, studying Santee, the dark eyes and crow-black hair, the hawklike face. 'You got some Injun in you?'

'Grandmother was a Choctaw. That make a difference?'

'Not to me. Just curious... What kinda work you do? If any.'

'Anything. I've been top hand on a West Texas spread, Alamo Smith's Busted S. I was foreman one winter up in Montana, I've busted broncs, hazed cows–'

'And thrown a wide loop once in a while?'

'Once in *long* while. When a man's hungry, his notions about right and wrong get kind of mixed up, Kirby.'

The sheriff grunted. 'And what's your hard-luck story...? You gotta have one. All you drifters got that way because the world kicked you in the ass and it's no fault of your own.'

Santee, still sitting in shadow on his bunk, lifted his face and the light washed over it. It was set in hard, sober planes. 'My hard luck started because I hit the booze.'

'Well, that's a change, havin' someone admit it. But you'd've had a good cause to hit the booze, wouldn't you?'

Santee's face hardened.

'If I did, it's no business of yours.'

Kirby didn't like that kind of sass, not from a man he was holding in his own cells.

'Well, sleep well, Santee. You might have a little company later on. Some boys from the Handy spread're in town and they tend to kick over the traces a mite. Could drop a couple of 'em in your lap – but then that's the kinda joint I run here.'

He smiled crookedly, turned on his heel and walked on back down the passage.

'Any supper?' called Santee after him but the lawman didn't answer.

They started dragging in the drunks about ten or eleven o'clock.

Santee was asleep with his battered hat covering his face when the first lot were shoved into the adjoining cell. Five of them, and there were only four bunks, so a shouting match started and it developed into a fight. More like a dance, Santee thought, as the drunken men swung wild punches, missed mostly, and staggered all around the cell, urged on by the ones not involved.

One of Kirby's deputies came down and ran a steel ladle along the bars, setting them to ringing so loudly that they all clapped their hands over their ears.

'Now – *shut up!*' bawled the cranky deputy, a blocky man with greying hair and a sour disposition. 'Any more and we come in there with the billies!'

He earned several mouthfuls of obscenities and curses but the drunks did shut down, some, the booze catching up with them, and slowly they dropped off to sleep.

An hour later they threw a single drunk into Santee's cell. The man staggered wildly and fell across the drifter who had the lower bunk – there were only two bunks in this cell. Santee shoved the man off and he

15

slipped and fell.

'Go sleep it off,' the drifter said without heat.

The man got to his feet, swaying, and Santee saw he was young – and, if he read the signs right, spoiling for trouble. He had an arrogant look about him, a high-bridged nose that he actually tilted back while he looked at Santee with bleak close-set deep-blue eyes. His hair was tousled, fair, and trimmed neatly around the neck and slim sideburns. The jaw was weak and the lips red and wet like a child's. What his clothes must have cost could have kept Santee from going hungry for a week.

'Judas priest!' he exclaimed, swinging towards the bars and stumbling. But he grabbed the uprights and clung to them, yelling loudly: 'Sheriff! *Sher-iff!* Goddamnit, Kirby, get on in here or Jed'll have Steve castrate you! *Get in here, damn you!*'

What surprised Santee was that Sheriff Kirby did saunter up to the door of the cell. Two men in the neighbouring cell were awake and watching sleepily now.

'The hell's wrong this time, Will?' the sheriff growled, barely glancing at Santee who was sitting up on the edge of his bunk now.

16

Without turning, Will threw out an arm, pointing in the drifter's direction. 'Him! *He's* what's wrong! How come you throwed me in here with a stinkin' drifter?'

Kirby saw Santee's shoulders stiffen. He made a small movement with his hand, indicating that the drifter should just stay calm. 'I admit he smells-up the place a little, Will, but this accommodation's the best I can offer tonight. Kept it specially for you. Knew you'd be in sooner or later.'

Will swayed, frowning, thinking about the lawman's words. 'You're bein' smart-ass, Kirby! I can tell! Don't think I won't tell Jed, neither!'

'Tell him what you like, Will. You're stayin' where you are till I decide to turn you loose. You owe Bink Daniels for that mirror you broke in his bar and Muffy Cadell says you busted up one of her gals. Judge Merton'll be back in town sometime tomorrow, so you get some rest. So's you'll be nice and fresh for court.'

Will blinked, blowing out his cheeks, then his face hardened and the slack red lips tightened. 'You ain't gettin' me in no court!'

'Told Jed last time that if I had to lock you up again, you were gonna face the judge, not just have him pay for your hell-pranks

17

on the quiet.'

'By God, we'll have your badge, Kirby!'

'Aw, go to sleep, Will.' Kirby glanced at Santee. 'Name's Will Handy. His father Jed owns the biggest spread in the valley. Got delusions of grandeur, aims to build an empire to leave this sorry son of a bitch of a son. You might like to get acquainted. Will can maybe put in a word for you if you check out OK, get you a job on the Flyin' H.'

Kirby winked and smiled crookedly and walked away, Will Handy calling after him. Then when it became apparent the sheriff wasn't paying any attention, Will turned and glared at Santee.

'Christ, a stinkin' half-breed into the bargain!' Will spat on the floor, stumbled across and spat again – this time on Santee's worn and scuffed boot. 'Git outta that bunk, 'breed! I don't like heights! *You* take the top one!'

Santee stood slowly, looking soberly at Handy. 'You're just a ray of sweetness and light, ain't you? Well, can see I ain't gonna get much sleep this night unless you get all tucked in first. So...'

Santee's fist barely moved six inches. It drove into Handy's midriff and the man lurched back two feet, jackknifing, gagging. Santee twisted his fingers in the tousled fair locks, yanked the contorted face up and hammered him on the jaw.

The deep-blue eyes crossed and then showed only the whites. Will's legs buckled and Santee ducked a shoulder into the man's mid-section, straightened and heaved him up onto the top bunk.

He dusted off his hands and stretched out on the bottom bunk again. A slurred voice from the next cell said,

'Man, you gonna die when he wakes up!'

'Well, it looks like it's the only way to get any peace around here. To hell with him. And you, too. Now pipe down and let me get some shut-eye.'

2
Payback

The men from the Flying H were still snoring when Abe Kirby sent in a deputy named Cropp. He was younger than the one Santee had seen last night, younger and unfriendly.

'Out,' he snapped as he opened the door of the cell, jerking his head at Santee who was starting to get up off the bunk.

Above him, Will Handy snored. There were drones and mutterings and grunts from the bunch piled into the cell next door.

In the passage, the deputy shoved Santee twice, impatiently, jerking a threatening hand to his gun-butt when the prisoner looked around, scowling.

'Don't gimme any trouble, drifter.'

Santee said nothing and was taken through a side door and a high wooden gate that led into an enclosed yard about ten feet square.

'Go work up an appetite,' growled the deputy and closed the gate.

Santee heard the bolt slap across and

21

looked around. The yard was bare except for a rain butt and he could make out worn criss-crossing paths where many feet had walked or run over the years. It was an exercise yard.

'Just what I need,' he breathed but stripped off his shirt and went to the rain butt which was half full of water that had insects floating on top. He skimmed them off with his cupped hand, rinsed his mouth, then scooped water over his arms and torso and lastly his head.

The chill brought him fully awake and he moved away from the wall's shadow into the slant of sunlight that reached down into the yard. As he dried, he looked around, then went back to the rain butt and washed his shirt, squeezing out the water. He was holding it in the sunlight when the door opened and Kirby himself came in.

'Want some breakfast?'

Santee nodded and walked across, following the sheriff into a back room behind the law offices. There were plates of bacon and eggs and fried cornpone on the table with a coffee-pot and two tin mugs. They sat down and began to eat.

'Sleep well?'

Santee scowled. 'Yeah. Thanks for the

company! And waking up to Deputy Smiler kinda put the gilt edge on it, you know what I mean?'

Kirby chuckled. 'Yeah, Cropp is kinda surly. Havin' woman trouble... I'll turn loose them drunks in a while.'

'Thought you were taking Will to court.'

Kirby scowled. 'His father moves fast. Seems someone got word to Jed last night that I had Will locked up. Sent this ramrod and trouble-shooter, Steve Bodie, in first thing and he squared away with the saloon and the cathouse. No charges.'

'Hard to fight a man with power and money.'

'They usually go together.' Kirby squinted at his prisoner. 'You slug Will?'

Santee shrugged. 'He needed to sleep it off.'

'Yeah. Well, you watch yourself. Will Handy don't forgive nor forget – and that's a hardcase outfit Jed runs. They been told to watch out for Will.'

Santee held the lawman's steady gaze. 'Won't bother me much if I'm being bars, will it?'

'Well – I'm still waitin' to make sure you ain't wanted for anythin', but Bink Daniels at the saloon says his swamper got drunk and fell down the trash pit, busted a collar bone. I'm willin' to let you work durin' the day to earn a dollar, but I'll lock you up at night till I get the all-clear on you. You gimme your word you won't run?'

'Yeah, you've got it.' Santee sounded suspicious; he wasn't used to lawmen showing a halfway decent streak towards him.

'You try to run out and next time I'll throw away the key.'

'I give my word, I stick by it.'

Kirby stared as he chewed the last of his bacon, then nodded jerkily.

Hell, he must be getting soft in his old age. For some reason he believed this drifter.

The Red River Saloon – original that! – wasn't the first saloon Santee had worked in as a swamper. He knew what to do and he did it – and a little extra, like stacking away spare chairs from last night's wingding and left in the passage behind the beaded curtain at one end of the bar. He found an empty room and stacked them in there, swept the dusty passage and picked up some papers that were scattered about.

Bink Daniels scratched at his thinning hair, which was plastered to his skull with some poop he'd made the mistake of buying from a snakeoil drummer. It was supposed to make your hair grow. All it did was make him look more bald and he was pretty damn certain he'd actually *lost* a few more strands since starting to use it.

'I just been lookin' for you – out in the yard behind the empties,' he told Santee. 'Usually find my swampers drainin' out the bottles. Guess you ain't a drinker.'

'Like a beer and a few redeyes as much as the next man. But not when I'm working.'

Daniels shook his head. 'Well, looks like I'm gonna get my money's worth outta you. Leave the passage here. I got some empty barrels lyin' around the yard. S'posed to've been stacked by my last man a week ago. Put 'em up agin the north wall. That's the one that–'

'I know my directions,' Santee said and leaned his whisk-broom against the wall, went out into the yard and found the barrels.

He rolled them closer to the wall and started to stack them two high. He was putting up the third one when a rough voice said behind him,

'Will you just look at that!'

Santee glanced over his shoulder as he settled the barrel into place, tensed when he saw four men standing there watching him.

One of them was Will Handy.

'Reckon he could be Samson?' someone asked and another said, spitting first,

'Nah. His hair ain't long enough.'

'But his nose is,' said Will Handy with a tight smile. 'Pokes it in where it ain't wanted. Ain't that right, 'Breed?'

'You're telling it, Will,' Santee said easily, sounding a lot more easy than he felt. His eyes watched them constantly and he stepped back when they came forward.

'Yeah, I'm tellin' it! You know why? Because I'm in charge round here! These boys work for Pa and they know they better do just like I say if they want to go on workin' for him...' He looked around him at the three hardcases, jerked his head at Santee. 'Teach this lousy drifter a lesson, fellers!'

Santee was as ready as he could be against three of them and as they closed, he ducked and weaved, getting away from the barrels, but not before he tipped one into them. Two men yelled as they fended off the heavy barrel and the other slipped. Will Handy looked alarmed and hurriedly stepped back.

Santee went after him and straight-armed him with a right that almost tore the kid's head off. Will staggered and by then the others were clear of the rolling barrel and coming in with fists swinging.

Santee danced aside and rammed the first man in the midriff, throwing his jacknifing body into the path of the others. Two collided but the other weaned around, clipped Santee along the side of the head. He stumbled, but came back with an elbow that took the advancing cowhand in the chest, just under the sternum. The man lifted to his toes, gagging, fighting for breath, red in the face. Santee helped him fall with a chopping hammerblow to the side of the neck.

Then the other two were on him, big, beefy range men, used to living rough and taking punishment. Santee dealt out as much as he could but they seemed to shake off his blows, kept crowding him back and worked him into a corner between the wall and the end of his line of barrels. He couldn't swing his arms properly, not even to cover up, and they hammered at him until the blood streaked his face and his legs wobbled. One of them rapped his head back against the curved hickory staves and iron hoops binding them. Santee saw shooting stars and bolts of lightning. There was thunder, too, as hard knuckles smashed against his head and body.

He lowered his head and tried to ram his way out by sheer brute force. But these men had their wind now and braced their solid legs, putting their shoulders into him so that he bounced back. They pinned him there and a knee took him in the belly. The breath burst out of him and the world turned red, shot through with yellow and black.

When he could see again, through a white haze, they had his arms spread against the wall, one man on each holding him immobile. The third ranny, a tree with clothes on, wiped a hand across blood-oozing nostrils, doubled up huge fists and went to work on him. Blow after blow sledged into his body, making his ribs creak and his guts turn to mush. A knee ground into his belly again and a head butted him in the face, breaking his nose. His eyes started to close and his legs wouldn't support him but the two cowboys held him upright.

The big man sucked at a split knuckle and looked at the bloody, ragged figure sagging between his two companions. His face was kind of handsome in a brutal sort of way, thick-lipped, eyes a bright blue, his naturally wavy hair the colour of ripe wheat, though dark around the edges with sweat right now. He turned to Will Handy who had been watching, bright-eyed, tensed.

'He's softened up now, Will. All yours.'

'Thanks, Steve,' Handy said, pushing his gun holster around to the back of his hip so it wouldn't be in the way.

Then he spread his boots, settled them firmly, worked his fingers and finally curled them into fists. But he uncurled one, twisted fingers in Santee's wet hair and jerked his head up and back, smashing his skull against the wall.

'Hey, 'breed! You in there? You hear me? You *better* damn well hear!' He shook Santee and the man groaned, eyes rolling in their puffy, bruised sockets. 'This is Will Handy speakin'. Remember the name, you son of a bitch! And next time you even *think* about layin' a hand on me, remember this!'

He started hammering a tattoo of blows into Santee's midriff, grunting, arms working wildly, out of rhythm in his excitement. He began to whine when he realized he wasn't inflicting as much punishment on Santee as he wanted to and the man with yellow hair stepped closer, saying,

'Get your rhythm right, kid! You're wearin' yourself out without hardly hurtin' him.

29

Stop a moment and I'll show you how—'

'He *better* stop! And you better step away from him, Steve!'

They spun at the cracking voice behind, turned to see Sheriff Abe Kirby standing there with a shotgun in his hands, thumb resting on the hammer-spur. Behind him, a worried-looking Bink Daniels ran a trembling hand over his pomaded hair.

'*I said get away from him!*' roared Kirby, cocking both hammers on the Greener and the men stepped back from Santee.

Released, he fell to his knees, put down his hands and stayed that way, head hanging, blood dripping onto the scuffed ground.

'You still with us, Santee?'

The battered man nodded without looking up and the sheriff ran his hard gaze over the four Flying H men. He let it settle on the yellow-haired man.

'Big Steve Bodie watchin' out for Jed Handy's brat again! Don't you ever get tired of wipin' his nose for him, Steve?'

'I do what I'm paid for,' Bodie said in a deep voice. 'An' you oughta know better'n to lock up Will with some 'breed drifter! Jed won't forget this.'

'I mayn't give him a chance to,' Kirby replied easily. 'Because this time I've caught

30

you red-handed and I aim to lock *all* of you up!'

The two cowhands looked alarmed. Will seemed uncertain and looked to Bodie who sneered at the lawman.

'Jed's lawyer'd have us out in an hour!'

'Not if the charge is attempted murder.'

'The hell you say!' snapped Bodie. 'You'd have a helluva job provin' that.' He looked coldly at Santee. 'If this 'breed knows what's good for him, he'll quit town while he can still walk – and then you won't have a case, Kirby.'

'What you say to that, Santee?' the sheriff asked and Wes Santee climbed slowly and painfully to his feet. Kirby winced when he saw the smashed nose and battered face and the bruised and torn flesh showing through the rents in the old shirt.

Santee wiped the back of a hand across his oozing nostrils, stared briefly at the red smears. He flicked his eyes first to Bodie then to Will Handy.

'I was stacking these here barrels,' he said sounding as if it was hard work even to talk. 'The stack collapsed on me … I was lucky these fellers happened along and pulled me out from under…'

Kirby's jaw dropped in astonishment at

31

Santee's words. Steve Bodie curled a thick lip.

'So you got enough brains to know which side your bread's buttered, huh, 'breed?'

'Yeah!' threw in Will Handy, getting back his confidence now. 'You're showin' some sense, 'breed! Just git outta town in the next hour and you won't have nothin' to worry about!'

'Shut up, Will,' growled Kirby, iron gaze boring into Santee. 'You don't want to charge these fellers with anythin'? Have I got it right?'

Wes Santee nodded, seeing the hostility in the lawman's face. 'An accident – I'm lucky to get off as lightly as I did.'

'That's right smart of you, feller,' Bodie said but he seemed a little puzzled – as if he couldn't *quite* believe Santee's attitude.

'But I won't be leaving town,' Santee said flatly and that brought them all up on their toes. 'I've got a job now – I need the money. I'll stick around for a while.'

'Listen, I told you...' started Will Handy, squeezing the words between his teeth.

'Leave it, Will,' Bodie said. 'Just – leave it. I think Santee knows better'n to tangle with Flyin' H again.'

Kirby suddenly spat in disgust, waved the

shotgun at the cowboys. 'Go on! Get the hell outta here! In fact, right outta town! I don't want to see none of you still in town in thirty minutes–' He flicked his gaze to Santee. 'And you – I'll point you in the direction of a sawbones and you can make your own way there. Come on! *Move!* All of you!'

They moved, Santee dragging along painfully. Sheriff Kirby followed them out on to Main, not speaking.

He touched Santee on the shoulder, pointed halfway along the block to where a doctor's shingle swayed on rusted chains in the hot breeze sweeping up from the river.

Then he heeled abruptly and strode away towards his office, disgust showing in his every movement.

Santee hobbled along the walk, folk giving his bloody form a wide berth.

3
One Man's Luck

Abe Kirby had calmed down by the time he got a reply to his wire to Yuma Territorial Prison. He walked into the cell block where Santee was stretched out on the lower bunk, reading a yellowed newspaper.

The door was open. He had spent the last two days here at the doctor's insistence and Kirby hadn't been pleased at the prospect but figured the man had to recuperate somewhere. Santee himself hadn't been too keen on the arrangement, either, but a couple of attempts at moving about and he had seen the wisdom of the doctor's orders.

Now he sat up on the edge of the bunk, folding the newspaper, bruises and cuts still evident, left eye swollen badly and surrounded by puffy, purple flesh. He looked at the easily-recognizable telegraph form in the lawman's hands and lifted his gaze to Kirby's face.

'You did your time in Yuma, all right. Sentence was six months, but you served nine.'

There was a query in the words and Santee said nothing for a few moments.

'Had a little trouble. Bought a jug of the moonshine some of the cons make from fruit and vegetable peelings. It was foul, so I sold it and the feller I'd bought it from figured I was trying to muscle in on his territory.'

'I hear they get a mite touchy about such things in the pen. What happened?'

'They set me up in the wash-house. He came at me with a knife.'

Santee went silent and Kirby waited, finally snapped, 'And…?'

'I took it away from him.'

'And skewered him.'

'Him or me.'

'Three months added to your sentence don't seem like much for killin' a man.'

'There were witnesses and seems he wasn't popular anyway, just mean. Warden said I did everyone a favour.'

'You were lucky. All right. I got no call to hold you any longer. Bink says he owes you a little money for the work you've done and the job's still open if you want it. He has a lean-to out back of the saloon you can use.'

Santee stood stiffly, just covering a wince. 'I'm obliged, Kirby. The law don't usually treat me so kindly.'

Kirby grunted. 'I generally take a man as I find him, but one thing I need to know: where'd you come from before you hit this place?'

He saw the wariness in Santee's battered face and Kirby tensed a little. There was some kind of guilt there...

'Just rode the rails up from San Antonio, stopping here and there, but couldn't find work...'

'Uh-huh.' Kirby knew he wasn't being told the whole truth. And he also knew the train Santee had come in on had made its last stop in Fort Worth. 'OK, you can stay here tonight, but you better decide if you're going back to work for Bink.'

'I'll work for him.'

When Santee was washing-up at the bench outside, the surly young deputy named Cropp came up to him and thrust a rolled faded blue shirt at him.

'Don't fit me any more,' he said curtly and started to turn away.

'Thanks.' Santee sounded – and looked – surprised.

Cropp paused, looking back over his shoulder. 'Anyone game enough to stand up agin Steve Bodie *and* Jed Handy's kid gets my vote.' He spat and moved on.

Santee watched him go, shaking his head a little, dried himself on a scrap of towel, patting carefully over the bruised ribs and midriff, then tried on the shirt. It fitted tolerably well and when he went to see Bink Daniels, the man handed him a pair of worn but serviceable Levis.

'Feller left 'em here a while back,' Daniels said, unconsciously patting his pomaded hair – which he did a hundred times a day and would have been surprised if anyone had told him so. He added with a wink, 'Lowers the tone of the place, havin' my swamper wearin' rags.'

Santee half smiled. 'Yeah, guess it does. Thanks, Bink.'

'Got a room full of old boots out back – piled up over the years. Pick 'em over later. You'll likely find a pair to fit.'

He could see that Santee was a little bewildered by this and added, gruffly, 'Jed Handy might have this town buffaloed, but he don't realize no one likes a man they're scared of. So when someone stands up to him...' He shrugged.

Santee said nothing and spent the rest of the afternoon scrubbing out the lean-to, stuffing old wet newspapers into the cracks in the walls and fixing the leather hinges on the rattly door. The bunk was crude, burlap nailed to a couple of saplings set in forked legs. Then Muffy Cadell, the woman who ran the cathouse next door to the saloon, sent one of her girls across with a couple of blankets.

The girl didn't look like the usual whore to Santee. She was pretty young for one thing, with nice, glowing skin, chestnut-haired, with a coltish look.

She said her name was Deborah.

'Muffy said if you want some extra work, she can use you.'

'Doing what?' Santee asked warily and the girl smiled, her whole young face lighting up.

'Cleaning up! What did you think...?'

He felt himself flushing a little and shrugged. Still smiling, she said, 'Muffy doesn't like Will Handy *or* Steve Bodie.'

'I'm beginning to think the whole town don't like anything about the Flying H.'

She sobered. 'You're probably right, but Will isn't so bad. Just – sort of confused. Trying to grow up too fast, and be like his father or Steve Bodie.'

Santee was amused by this young whore's

diagnosis of Will Handy. Hell, Will could probably shade her a year or two...

The stiffness and soreness passed over the next few days as he got on with his job. Then Muffy Cadell hired him to sweep out a room she was going to decorate and turn into a 'special parlour – she said – and to give it a general renovation. She was fortyish with a fine figure and a pleasant face marred only by a coldness lurking in her wide-set eyes.

'Can you handle that?'

'Sure, but I'm no expert.'

She nodded. 'There'll be some painting, too, and there's a couple of floorboards need tearing up and replacing. I'll pay you twenty dollars.'

It was a long time since Santee had seen twenty dollars all at once, especially coming out of his own pocket.

He was working on one of the floorboards the next night – hammering and sawing didn't seem to bother Muffy's clientele – when he heard raised voices in the passage outside, Muffy's and a man's among them.

'Look, just leave her alone, Bo! I don't allow my girls to be roughed up, you know that. Now just leave her be and get the hell out of here! I don't want to see you in here again!'

The last word was cut short as there was the unmistakable sound of a hand striking flesh. A woman cried out in alarm more than pain and Santee, already moving towards the door, knew it hadn't been Muffy – she wasn't the screaming type.

'Bo' turned out to be one of the hardcases who had held him while Bodie worked him over. Muffy was bent over, holding her face, reddened on one side by Bo's brutal hand. The man himself had turned to the other woman, who was wearing only a light gown, now torn and revealing most of her charms. She was cowering as Bo, obviously drunk and mean, moved in on her, fist raised. She was the one who had screamed. Her face was already reddened from previous blows and her lower lip was cut.

Santee reognized Deborah.

He lunged forward and caught Bo's raised hand, twisted hard, and the man grunted in pain as the movement brought him spinning around. His reddened eyes flew wide when he recognized Santee and he snarled, threw a punch. Santee dodged easily and then, careful of his still swollen nose, smashed his forehead into Bo's face.

Blood spurted and Bo howled, fell back against the wall. Then he thrust away, swearing, the lower half of his face dripping blood as he swung two fast, hurting blows into Santee's damaged ribs. He grunted and one leg buckled and Bo aimed a fist at his face. Santee ducked under the arm, ripped a hammering blow into the man's midriff and as he doubled over, brought up his knee. Bo grunted, slammed into the wall and, shaking his head, grabbed for his gun. Santee stepped forward and swung a boot at the man's knee. It was a good solid boot, one of a pair he had found in Bink's spare room, and it fitted really well. Bo howled aloud, and collapsed, writhing, holding his injured leg, sobbing in extreme pain. Santee reached for his dirty shirt-collar, dragged him down the passage, past a staring crowd in the foyer-bar of the cathouse, and threw him out of the front door. Bo rolled into the gutter, limbs flailing loosely, almost passing out with pain.

Santee kicked him in the head and Bo slumped in the slush of the gutter.

He went back inside, where several whores stared at him as he went back down the passage to where Muffy was holding a wet cloth against her face – apparently brought by Deborah who was clutching the torn robe awkwardly across her body.

'Go get cleaned up Deborah,' Muffy said, her eyes on Santee, and as the girl moved away silently, she added to Santee, 'Maybe I should've hired you as bouncer – I sent my man out on an errand and Bo took advantage of it.'

Santee shook his head. 'Not in my line. But I kind of owed Bo.'

'He'll be lucky if he walks again without a stick! I sure hope I never cross you up, Wes Santee!'

'I've won a lot of fights, and I've lost a few. Losing doesn't bother me, but I don't like it when I'm being held while someone else beats on me.'

'No-o. Poor Deborah. She's my youngest and has to put up with a lot of abuse. All the cowhands ask for her.'

'Why doesn't she leave?'

'She makes good money.' Muffy sounded defensive.

'There's got to be more to it than that.'

'If there is, it's her business. Thanks for your help.'

An hour later, she came down to the room where he was working and handed him a gun rig: a cartridge-belt with every loop filled, wrapped about an oiled-leather holster containing a used but cared-for Colt pistol.

'Belonged to my husband. Why're you looking like that? Even whorehouse-keepers get married. Anyway, he's long gone. I had it oiled and cleaned. You'll be needing it if you keep on treading on Jed Handy's toes.'

Santee buckled on the rig. It felt strange, for it was months since he had worn a six-gun. He settled it comfortably on his hip and nodded his thanks.

'It could come in right handy.'

She smiled. 'I think it just might.'

Santee hadn't had as much good luck for a coon's age. Plenty of the bad kind had been dogging him for the past couple of years, but he didn't want to think about that right now.

He preferred to think about his present situation. Things seemed to be changing for the better. Hell, he hadn't been so well off in months. Two jobs, decent clothes and boots, even a good gun-rig. He had taken it outside of town, to a dry wash just above the ferry on the north side of the river, and put it through its paces. The action was smooth and someone had worked on the trigger, made it a shade lighter than he preferred, but he wasn't going to gripe about that. It was about as accurate as the average Colt Frontier model and with a little work on the blade foresight and the sighting channel on the topstrap it might improve some but what the hell? A sixgun wasn't made for long-distance accuracy.

It was most effective if you got within eight or ten feet of your target and blew it to hell. Sure, some men worked on the bullet-weights and powder-loads and shot amazing groups on targets but the average Colt wasn't designed for that kind of work, either. It was mighty handy if you ran up against a grizzly with a grouch or a rattler ready to sink its fangs into you or your horse, and it was a comfort to have if a man got into an argument that went beyond the usual name-calling, but it wasn't meant for much more than that.

Anyway, he sure was comforted by it. But Abe Kirby hadn't seemed all that pleased when he had visited him in the lean-to a couple of days after Muffy Cadell had presented him with the gun.

'I hope you got no notions of usin' that around my town.'

'Not unless I have to.'

'Take my advice, *don't* have to. Just stay outta the way of Flying H.'

'I won't be going looking for 'em.'

'Good. Friend of mine is sheriff in Fort Worth. Believe you met him. Pack Marney.'

Santee was wary now. 'We – said "howdy".'

'You said more'n that!'

Santee stared at the lawman, sighed. 'So you been sending more wires. I didn't start that fight.'

'Mebbe not, but you sure ended it.'

'The hell was I s'posed to do? Stand still while that Mexican slipped his *cuchillo* under my ribs?'

'Guess not. Pack says he was a touchy type, already drunk when you spilled his drink for him. That's all that kept you outta jail. You seem to like knives?'

'No. Can use 'em well enough for butchering game or beef or whittling or cutting leather. They're a fine tool, but there's something about cold steel slicing into warm flesh that gives me goosebumps.'

'But not enough to keep you from usin' a blade.'

Santee's gaze didn't waver. 'Not when I have to.'

Kirby scratched at his moustache. 'I dunno, Santee. I was willin' to give you a break, but you're just a piece of hell looking for some place to happen.'

Santee's mouth tightened. 'Kirby, I'm obliged for what you've done, and how folk have treated me around here. I don't look for trouble, but it does have a habit of finding me. I'll move on if you want. But I'd be obliged if you'd give me long enough to finish painting that room for Muffy. I can use the twenty bucks she's promised me.'

'How long?'

'Another couple days.'

'Make it sundown two days from now. There's a train leaves around then for points north. I'll come down and wave you off.'

So things hadn't changed for the better after all!

Then Bo tried to kill him.

He lurked in the shadows behind Muffy's place – called The Dovecot – waiting for Santee to make his nightly journey from the lean-to through the sagging gate in the fence into the yard of the cathouse. Here he would pick up his paint-cans and brushes and turpentine from the tool shed then go in the back door and start work on the room.

Bo had been using a walking-stick since Santee had kicked him and there was a leather support laced around the leg which made it hard to bend. It ached interminably and he didn't get much sleep and Jed Handy had told him he was stopping his pay until he could work again.

Bo simply *couldn't* do any worthwhile chore and hanging around the bunkhouse all day gave him a lot of time to brood. Too much time…

Steve Bodie had been egging him on to do something about Santee, and Bo had enough sense to know Steve's urging had been on the orders of Jed himself. The rancher didn't take kindly to his son's being manhandled by any 'breed drifter and although he was by no means afraid of Abe Kirby, Jed did have respect for the tough lawman.

So, after Santee had kicked Bo's kneecap loose he had seen a chance to get back at the goddamned 'breed by using Bo. And Bo was in enough pain to do what Jed wanted – but not for nothing. He'd braced himself with a couple of good snorts of redeye before going to see the rancher in his office.

Jed Handy wasn't a big man but he gave the impression of size simply because of his overpowering – some said bullying – personality. Handy was a rancher of the old school, a man who had fought Indians and dust storms and floods and drought and dug in his heels and claimed all of Beaumont Valley. When the town had developed from a ferry-stop and trading post and expanded, he had been forced to cut back his grazing land some. Then he'd had more than his share of trouble fighting with the Butterfield Stageline during the short time it operated, and when it had finally closed down, he'd thought that was an end to it.

Then that damn railroad, The Katy, came through and turned Jed's hair grey and gave him an ulcer and he had to move back Flying H's boundaries even more. But he swore one day he'd have the whole damn valley back – it was *his*, goddamnit! He'd fought for it, opened up this country, and he would have it again before he died. And Will and his future wife and family would have something worthwhile to look forward to.

He was a sour man, without humour, his ulcer eating at him because he fed it with the simmering anger that dwelt within him against every man, woman and child who lived in Beaumont Flats or who farmed any part of the valley.

Now he snapped his head up as Bo limped in, using his stick. He glared his annoyance at being interrupted while doing his book-work and Bo licked his dry lips, wondering what insanity had brought him here to try a shakedown on this butt-headed rancher. Too late to back out now.

'Jed, I'm goin' after that 'breed.'

'That's your business.' Handy said, making it clear it had nothing to do with him.

'Well – partly, I guess. But I'd be doin' you a favour, too, wouldn't I? Gettin' rid of him, squarin' away what he done to Will at the same time?'

'Don't you throw my son's name in my face. You got a chore to do, I don't want to know about it unless it's range work on Flyin' H.'

'OK. But I'm near crippled, Jed. Gonna be a few more weeks before I can get back to work and I'll be broke by then. If we could sort of – negotiate some kinda fee – I could take care of Santee and drift on. Then you could tell Kirby you fired me and that way it'd look even more like you had nothin' to do with the 'breed gettin' killed.'

Handy sat back in his chair, ran a hand through his silver-grey hair, scratched at the stubble on his square jaw. The eyes were cold and grey. 'If you *did* kill Santee, because of what he did to *you*, mebbe I could come up with some sort of severance pay to see you through for a spell...'

'How much?'

'It would depend on how well you did the job. No arguments, Bo! Take it or leave it.'

Bo took it, of course, and now he lifted his Colt and steadied it as Santee came through the gate in the fence, briefly silhouetted against the lights in the saloon.

Then a voice called from the upper floor rear window of The Dovecot: 'Wes! Watch out!'

Old instincts took over, and he went down on to one knee, the sixgun coming up and blasting at the glint of light on gun-metal in the shadows. Bo triggered and the shots blended as he jerked back, arms flailing. Santee shot again and splinters flew from the door as Bo spun into the woodwork and fell face down. Then the rear door slammed open and light washed into the yard as two men jostled and shouldered outside, guns in hand – Bo's back-up, arranged earlier – just in case.

Santee ducked when the first man fired at him and he threw himself prone as the second man triggered, too.

Wes Santee's Colt bucked in his hand, and the shots sounded like one long roar, as both men went down hard, bodies and falling guns clattering in the passageway. As the echoes died away, others, pushing into the passage to see what was going on, turned and fought to get back out of the line of fire.

But it was over.

Santee stood and walked forward, cocked and smoking gun covering the downed men. Bo was dead. One of the others wouldn't see another sun-up – he was the man who had held Santee while Bodie beat him. The third man was sprawled against the wall, breathing hard, eyes wide, holding a hand to his bleeding chest.

It was Will Handy.

Santee lowered his gun-hammer, ejected the used shells and swiftly and deftly reloaded. He was putting the gun back into his holster when Abe Kirby arrived with his shotgun and angrily arrested him.

It looked like his run of good luck had come to an abrupt end.

4
All Hell

Abe Kirby placed his hands on his hips and glared through the bars of Santee's cell.

'Make yourself at home, boy. You're gonna be there for a long time now.'

'The hell you talking about, Kirby?' Santee came lunging for the bars and the sheriff stepped back, but without any real show of alarm. 'It was self-defence. Bo was laying for me and he had back-up–'

'One of which was Will Handy, for Chrissakes! Judas, Santee, how the hell d'you *do* it! Jed Handy's son! That makes three out of the four who beat up on you. Now you tell me how that looks!'

'Don't care how it looks. Bo was laying for me! Hell, ask Deborah. She was the one called a warning from an upstairs window.'

The sheriff sighed and came a little closer to the bars, speaking more quietly now. 'I've spoken to her. She's not sure if Bo was *in* the outhouse or comin' out when he spotted you and grabbed the chance to take a shot at you.'

Kirby almost spat. 'And Will Handy and the other *hombre*–'

'Jace McCormack. He's dead.'

'Yeah, well I won't lose any sleep over that. But he and Will just *happened* to be coming out of the door at that time? Gimme a break, Kirby! It was a set-up and you're blind if you can't see it.'

The sheriff moved even closer to the bars. 'I'll tell you what I see, Santee – I see you've killed two men who held you while Steve Bodie beat you. You've wounded Will Handy and there's a good chance he won't pull through. You're a drifter, an ex-jailbird, and you're hell on wheels. A deaf, dumb and blind jury could find you guilty of murder!'

Santee's dark eyes narrowed. 'You're scared of Jed, ain't you?'

Kirby's mouth clamped into a razor slash, but he said softly, 'If Will dies, Jed'll rip this valley up stone by stone and clapboard by clapboard. He'll make the Red River live up to its name! And we – the folk who live in Beaumont Flats – are gonna be right in the middle!' He shook his head. 'Because of some hardcase drifter with his ass hanging out of his trousers! No, sir! Not if I can help it!'

Santee was caught flatfooted by the sheriff's words. He couldn't think of anything to say for a few seconds and by that time Kirby was storming away down the passage towards the front office. Santee stepped up to the bars and rattled the door in its frame.

'Damn you, Kirby! You ain't throwing me to the wolves!' But he knew that's exactly what Kirby was going to do.

There was no reply, of course. Unless you counted the slamming of the office door: it was a kind of punctuation-mark. Like a full stop.

Deborah Hatfield didn't feel so good. She was scared and she wasn't quite sure why.

She had warned Wes Santee and was glad she had – she owed him for taking on Bo the other night and she didn't care what anyone said. But Muffy Cadell took her aside after the dead and dying had been taken out of the Dovecot's backyard.

'Deborah, dear, I know why you did it, but you forgot what I've taught you, what I teach all my girls – never, but never poke your nose into other folk's business.'

'But Wes saved me from a working-over by Bo...'

Muffy held up her hand, unsmiling. 'I was there, remember? That was a fine thing Santee did, but that has nothing to do with what happened in our back yard–'

'Of course it does! I–'

Deborah reeled as Muffy slapped her across the face, not really hard, but the blow was so unexpected that the young girl staggered and blinked in shock, putting a hand to her reddening cheek.

'Let's not forget who runs things around here, Deborah, my dear,' Muffy said casually. 'I said: what happened with Santee and Bo had nothing to do with what happened in our yard. *It had nothing to do with us,* is what I mean.'

Tears welled in Deborah's eyes. 'I couldn't just let Bo shoot Wes down in cold blood!'

Muffy sighed. 'I know, dear, I know. But you could have dropped a bottle or a chamber-pot out of the window and stayed out of sight. See what I mean? Don't get the Dovecot involved! Now all the valley knows that Deborah Hatfield saved Santee's life – and thereby caused the death of Bo, Mc-Cormack – and now Will Handy.'

Deborah gasped, fingers going to her mouth. 'Will – died?'

'Half an hour ago. Never regained con-

sciousness. Now you see why I'm upset!'
Muffy Cadell's face was pale and there was
real worry in her eyes. 'All hell's going to
break loose in this valley, Deborah, you take
my word for it. Jed Handy worshipped Will,
had big plans for him and the Flying H.
He's not going to be satisfied with just
killing Wes Santee – he's going to want to
make every man, woman and child in town
suffer.'

'But – why? They had nothing to do with
Will's death!'

'They've been treating Santee pretty good
– finding him work, giving him clothes –
Jesus, *I* gave him the *gun!* To Jed's way of
thinking that puts folk on Santee's side and
someone's going to pay for it. *Everyone* is
going to pay for it. Including us! He'll likely
burn the Dovecot down around me! And all
because you felt beholden to Santee!'

Deborah knew now why she felt so sick
inside.

She suddenly tilted her head. 'Well, I *was*
beholden to him, Muffy! I'm glad I warned
him in time! I mean that! I'm *glad* I warned
him!'

Muffy Cadell grabbed the girl's arm and
Deborah cried out in pain, writhing, trying
to prise her fingers away from her flesh.

Muffy shook her.

'You see how glad you are when Jed sends Steve Bodie and half a dozen Flying H hands to see you! Think it gets rough on a Saturday night? Hell, dear, that's a Sunday-school picnic to what they'll do to you...'

'You're – you're just trying to frighten me!' Deborah's face was bloodless now and she was shaking.

'Damn right I'm trying to frighten you! And if you've got any sense you'll believe every word I say. Look, Jed Handy is working up to taking over the bank, our own Red River Trust. The word is that after this round-up, he'll have enough to buy out the other stockholders, lock, stock and barrel.'

'I don't know why he'd want to, but they – they mightn't want to sell to him.'

Muffy smiled thinly. 'Steve Bodie'll see they *want* to, all right.'

'Well – why does Mr Handy want the bank?'

'Girl, whoever owns the bank, owns the valley! He can run folks any way he wants once he's in control of their money. Then it'll be God help us all.'

'What's it got to do with me?'

'You're a part of it now, like it or not. Suppose you gave evidence at Santee's trial that you saw Bo waiting in ambush for Wes ... and the jury let him off because he was meant to be the victim? Folk would see that as a victory over Jed. Not a big one, but it would be a start – and Jed won't chance that.'

'And if I don't give my evidence? What happens to Wes Santee then?'

Muffy sighed. 'What's going to happen to him anyway, Deborah. Just a little sooner, that's all. The man killed Jed Handy's son. Nothing's going to save him, not you, not a court trial, nor anything else. Even if some of us would like to help him, we can't risk it. We have to *live* here, and do the best we can to survive.'

'But Wes can make a difference in this town! He's not afraid to stand up to Handy!'

'And look where it's landed him. You're right, dear, he *could* be good for this town but only if we're prepared to pay the price and I'm not alone in thinking it's way too high! Now, the best thing you can do is save your own neck. If you're out of town, Jed won't bother with you. He'll have Bodie take care of Santee.'

'No! I won't do it! I – I can't – *won't* – put him in that situation!'

'Honey, he's *already* in it, can't you see

that? Look, you have some money coming. I'll double it and you be on the night train out of here or I won't be responsible for what happens to you – I mean it! Now, start packing!'

Jed Handy stood on the rim of the canyon, staring out at the thunderheads way over near the horizon. He had been that way for over three hours now and Steve Bodie was growing restless.

Will Handy had died in his father's arms in the town infirmary without even opening his eyes. Jed's face, always carved in stone, turned even harder and more grim, as he drew the sheet up over his son's now-relaxed face.

'This will be the biggest funeral this valley has ever seen,' Handy said in a steady, firm voice. He turned to the stooped old doctor. 'You see Gillespie and tell him to make it the best – not the best he can, the goddamn *best!* Never mind the expense. Dust off that glass-sided hearse he's got stashed away in his barn. It's never used because folk round here can't afford it, but I can. And I want it for my boy. Come with me, Steve.'

He had stormed out to where their mounts were hitched and where some of the

Flying H crew had gathered, waiting for news. Jed gave it to them straight.

'Will's dead. It's gonna be a big funeral. Everyone in town and the goddamn valley is gonna be there. No excuses! You boys start ridin' and spread the word. Do whatever you have to, but you make certain-sure everyone's gonna come. Tell 'em anyone refuses, they'll have their place burned down.'

'Judas, Jed,' spoke up Drury, the wrangler. 'Kirby won't stand for that.'

Handy's look seemed to wither the young bronc-buster. 'Never mind Kirby – or anyone else. You follow my orders, and let me worry about the rest. Now get ridin'.'

Then he had led Steve out of town to the rim of Sawtooth Canyon.

And he had been standing there ever since, just staring at the horizon.

Itching to be doing something, Bodie walked across and stood beside Handy. He blinked when he saw dampness on the leathery old cheeks and Jed hurriedly wiped a hand across his face, swearing a little.

'Goddamn flies, they're everywhere – get in the corner of a man's mouth, his eyes...'

'Yeah, can drive a man loco,' Bodie agreed, looking away now. He had been shaken some

61

to know that the old man could shed a tear, even for Will. 'Jed, we best start fixin' things so's we can take care of this drifter.'

Handy continued to look out at the darkening thunderheads. 'He's a dead man walkin', Steve.'

'Yeah, but that's it – he *is* still walkin'. If I know Kirby, he'll be gettin' things ready for a trial and with that whore tellin' about how Bo was lyin' in ambush–'

'She's not tellin' nobody nothin'.' The rancher swung his bullet-like eyes towards his ramrod. 'You see to that.'

'Sure, no trouble, Jed, but we got to get by Kirby.'

'Yeah. Well, *I* want to see this 'breed who murdered my son!' Jed Handy rounded abruptly and strode towards his horse, a big, heavy-chested black with a wild eye. He swung up into saddle, feeling a stab of pain in his left shoulder, running down his arm, and recognizing it as a warning of angina – he had already survived one heart attack. Angrily, he wrenched the big head around, raked with his spurs and started back towards town while Bodie was still sprinting towards his own horse. When he caught up to the rancher, Jed turned to glare at him.

'You shoulda stopped Will!'

'I tried, Jed! Jesus, I *tried!* But you know what Will was like – he's got your stubborn streak. He wanted to get a chance at Santee and that was it.'

'You shoulda stopped him.'

Bodie swore under his breath. This was just great! Now Jed was laying the blame on him.

Still, that was typical enough of the rancher: he always looked around for some-one to blame for any scrapes Will got him-self into. Only this time, not even Jed Handy could do anything about what had hap-pened.

Which meant he would be mean as a wounded grizzly, striking out blindly at anyone and anything within reach.

He hoped Beaumont Flats realized all hell was about to break loose in this valley.

'So you're the son of a bitch who killed my boy!'

Santee didn't get up from the bunk as Jed Handy glared his hate at him through the cell-door bars.

'And you're the son of a bitch who sent him to kill me – and he couldn't do it, even with Bo and Jace to help.'

Handy actually kicked the barred door in his anger and snapped his head around to

Steve Bodie who was lounging against the passage wall. 'Get the key and drag that bastard out here!'

'No key!'

They all looked quickly towards the voice. Sheriff Kirby stood just inside the door leading to the front office, holding his shotgun. He walked forward slowly.

'You want to talk, do it through the bars.'

'Who the hell you think you're talkin' to, Kirby?' snapped the rancher. 'You offended me by makin' me and Steve leave our guns in the front office, but by Godfrey, you stand there with a cocked shogun pointin' at my belly and I swear I'll have your damn badge!'

'Swear all you like, Jed, but I don't trust you nor your damn ramrod. I'm stayin' here long as you stay. You don't like it, why, go.' Kirby jerked his head vaguely towards the street.

Jed's eyes slitted. 'I won't forget this, Kirby!'

'Never for a moment figured you would, Jed. Look, Santee's my prisoner. I'm investigatin' what's happened and he'll be brought to trial. And a jury'll decide what happens to him. It's called due process and God help us all if we throw it out of the window.'

Handy continued to glare at the sheriff a moment longer, then turned towards Santee and spat through the bars. 'You're a dead man, drifter!'

'Easy on the threats, Jed!' Kirby said curtly but Handy shouldered past him roughly. Steve Bodie followed, pausing to say to the lawman,

'You just made the biggest mistake of your life, Kirby.'

'No, Steve. My biggest mistake was not killin' you on the several occasions when I had the chance. Now get your boss outta town and stay out till the trial's over.'

'Don't believe you can enforce that, Kirby.'

'May not be on the books, but you just watch me do it.'

Bodie shrugged and moved on through to the front office where Handy waited impatiently. Kirby watched them leave and then turned back to Santee.

'Don't nothin' ever faze you?'

Wes Santee looked genuinely surprised. 'What? A few threats? Hell I've been threatened by experts and I'm still here. Jed Handy – nor Bodie – don't bother me.'

'Well, they ought to.'

'They bother you?'

'Some. Look, Santee, I – I figured I could head off trouble for the town by gettin' you into court and takin' a chance on a trial by jury. I kind of had a word with Muffy and she's agreed to get young Deborah outta town...'

Santee crossed to the bars in two long strides, face hard. 'She's the only one saw what happened! The only one can back up my story!'

Kirby nodded, uncomfortable. 'Yeah – well, I admit I figured maybe throwin' you to the wolves would save everyone a lot of hell but ... can't do it, Santee. I've stood up agin two lynch mobs when I could've made a lot of money just by findin' somethin' to do outta town for a few hours. I've been tempted, wouldn't be human if I hadn't, I guess, but – well, I may be old fashioned, but what it comes down to is I took an oath of office and I've tried to live up to it. Handy's a mighty big thorn in my side, in the side of everyone in Beaumont Valley for the matter of that, and givin' him you wouldn't solve a thing – he'd still tear this place up until he has it under this thumb.'

'You did kind of disappoint me earlier when you hinted you was gonna throw me to him,' Santee admitted. 'I had you figured for a decent man behind that star.'

Abe Kirby flushed a little. 'Well, I try to be. Some men let a star change 'em, make 'em forget they're men first, policemen somewhere down the line. But I ain't all that much of an angel. I ain't throwing you to Handy, but I ain't keepin' you around, neither. You're a one-man riot, Santee, and I don't need you in my town.'

Santee frowned. The sheriff added, hard-eyed,

'You're ridin' outta here on the night train to Wichita. Roughin' it in a boxcar won't be nothin' strange for you and you can get off anywhere you like – long as its at least a day's ride from here.'

Santee's face was hard. 'I get it. If I'm out of town, Handy won't cut loose: the son of a bitch'll come after me!' He waited for an answer but Kirby merely thrust out his jaw and tilted it, although his cheeks still burned some. 'Sure, you salve your conscience and save the town a heap of trouble, Handy gets a chance at me – and I get to go on the dodge. With no more than a few dollars to help me.'

'Look on the bright side. At least you'll have a gun.'

5
Return to Danger

Kirby was as good as his word. After dark he smuggled Santee out of the cell block and down to the railway siding by the unlit back streets of Beaumont Flats.

He had arranged with the guard in the caboose to look the other way while Santee climbed into an empty boxcar.

'I don't want to see you again, Santee,' the sheriff said gruffly, handing the drifter his gun-rig, the cartridge-belt wrapped around the holster which held the Colt. 'It's not loaded. And I don't want you to load it before I leave.'

The lawman's shotgun swung up casually as Santee took the rig and buckled it about his waist: he smiled thinly, looking down on Kirby.

'I guess I've got a few things to thank you for, Kirby.'

'Nope – I've done nothin' I wouldn't do for anyone else I figured needed a break. Just you make the most of it.'

'I aim to.' Santee stooped and offered his right hand. *'Adios,* Kirby.'

The sheriff nodded, made no move to take his hand, and started the heavy door closing along its slide. Santee watched as the gap narrowed swiftly and then the lawman was gone and he was left in the darkness of the boxcar.

He struck a vesta and lit the stub of candle Kirby had supplied. There was also a small sack of grub and his own warbag. Some straw in one corner would be spread out to make a bed. Santee sat down on his warbag, reloaded the Colt, then took out the sack of tobacco and papers he had bought and made a cigarette. Outside, he could hear the muted sounds of preparation for the train to move; the guard's voice calling *'Boooo-aaaarrrd!'* and then the wail of the loco's whistle, the thud of the steam slamming the pistons in their cylinders for the first time, rapidly becoming a tattoo that faded into a speedy rhythm and the clash of the coup-lings taking up the slack between the cars as the train lurched and began its long journey north.

He had built his cigarette but hadn't yet fired it up. He carefully smoothed the slim paper-and-tobacco cylinder between his fingertips and dropped it into his shirt pocket. He pinched out the candle stub and placed it beside the cigarette, then stood, moving his feet to steady himself as he picked up his warbag and went to the sliding door. He opened it a crack and the thunder of the train reached him with the coolness of the night. He was holding the door just wide enough for him to squeeze through and he watched the bushes sliding by in a grey blur, saw the wooden poles that supported the water-tanks, and next, more brush, but a little scattered now, then the bare grey earth of the embankment beyond the edge of town. He waited another couple of minutes and when the brush thickened and grew closer to the tracks, he jumped into the night.

Long experience had taught him how to relax and land safely, tumbling forward or sideways, depending on the terrain, sliding onto his back so he could use his boot-heels to slow his fall.

He lay there until the lights of the train had faded around the bend before the bridge across the river, then, stood and dusted himself down.

Slinging the warbag over his shoulder, checking that his gun was still safely holstered, he started walking back towards the distant lights of the town.

He had just reached the water-tanks when a figure stepped out from behind one of the thick uprights and blocked his path. Santee dropped his warbag. There was a whisper of metal sliding out of leather and his Colt hammer clicked back before the gun came up into line.

'Don't shoot, Wes! It's only me – Deborah Hatfield!'

Jed Handy kept a suite of rooms at the Beaumont Arms which he used whenever he stayed in town overnight or for a few days while settling some business deal.

He had arranged for his men to meet him there and was just finishing supper when eight cowboys, including Bodie, crowded in. Jed tossed down his glass of wine, dabbed at his leathery lips and ran his humourless eyes over the group. 'You do what I said?' he barked and most of the men looked at Steve Bodie, silently electing him spokesman.

'It's done, Jed. We seen everyone in town and told 'em to attend Will's funeral two days from now. The undertaker'll have the hearse all varnished and spick'n'span on time and I made the preacher cancel a couple of Christenin's so's you can hold the service.'

Handy nodded, his eyes still showing no pleasure. 'You tell 'em they're to line the route to the ranch and then come out while we plant Will in the ground next to his ma and two brothers?'

'They know what they gotta do, Jed – and they know what'll happen if they don't.'

'All right.' He stepped forward and took a chamois drawstring poke from his pocket, opened it and spilled its contents across a small table. Gold coins glittered in the lamp light. 'Go have yourselves a night on the town. You can stay over if you want and go back to the spread in the mornin'. Not you, Steve. You and me've got a chore to do.'

Bodie showed no disappointment, in fact he was half smirking as he watched the cowboys grab a gold five-dollar piece each and then hurry out, muttering *Gracias, boss*'.

When they had gone, Steve held Handy's jacket for the old man who shrugged into it with a small grunt when his rheumatism twinged his shoulders.

'Law-office, Jed?'

Handy nodded, opened a desk drawer and took out an old-fashioned pepperpot five-barrelled pistol. The barrels were loaded with powder and shot and Jed quickly thumbed percussion caps he took from a small round tin onto the nipples. The gun had belonged to his father and it had served Jed well on several occasions – and would again.

He dropped the gun into his pocket, Steve Bodie held open the door and they went out and downstairs into the street, crossed over to the law office and found Abe Kirby just finishing a meal at his desk, a stained napkin tucked into his shirt-collar. He glanced up at his visitors, took off the napkin and wiped his mouth and chin which showed a few traces of chilli sauce, then reached for his coffee-mug.

'Visitin' me twice in the same day,' he said unsmiling. 'Must be one for the books.'

'You hear about Will's funeral?' Handy snapped. The lawman nodded.

'Yeah. Hear you've got the whole damn town buffaloed.'

'Everyone's comin' – except you.'

Kirby shrugged. 'I aimed to be there – still do.'

Jed Handy seemed to relax some. 'Well, sure. That's fine. Makes everyone in town *and* the valley.'

Kirby seemed as if he was going to comment but refrained, drained his coffee. He stood, reaching for his hat. Steve Bodie moved in such a way that his big body was now between the sheriff and the rack where he kept his shotgun. Kirby looked at him coldly.

'Step aside, Steve.'

Bodie ignored him. 'We want to see Santee.'

Kirby's eyes narrowed. 'You already seen him.'

'Jed wants to ask him somethin' he forgot this afternoon.'

'Come back in the mornin'. I've got my rounds to do – Cropp's havin' so much trouble with his wife I've give him the night off, and Benbow's down with a bellyache. Means I have to do everythin' myself – and that don't give me time to stand watch while you two visit Santee.'

'You don't have to. We ain't gonna do anythin' to him,' Jed Handy said, watching Kirby closely, suspiciously. He started for the door that led to the cell block. 'We know our way, Abe.'

Kirby reached around Bodie hurriedly and grabbed at his shotgun but the ramrod, sensing something was wrong here, blocked him, snatched up the gun himself. Both cowmen were startled when Kirby whipped up his sixgun and laid the barrel across Bodie's head. The man staggered, falling to one knee. Kirby grabbed the Greener, swung the barrels to cover both men.

'Get away from that door, Jed!'

Handy turned slowly, his face hard and beginning to cloud with rising rage as Bodie staggered to his feet and leaned groggily against the wall.

'By hell! I hope you ain't done what I got me a suspicion you have Abel.' Kirby said nothing and Handy swore. 'You have, ain't you! You've turned that son of a bitch loose!'

'He didn't know it was Will, Jed – just saw someone tryin' to kill him and he shot first. Any man would. Not sense in putting the County to the expense of a trial when you know ahead of time the man's innocent.'

The words reached Bodie's reeling brain and he stumbled towards Kirby but froze when the gun swung in his direction. 'You damned fool!' he slurred, rubbing at the rising welt on his left temple. 'Santee was ours!'

'No – he was my prisoner. I had nothing to hold him on. So I turned him loose. You better not go lookin' for him. I won't stand for any rigged gunfights in my town.'

Jed Handy was breathing hard, nostrils white-rimmed, his pupils so shrunken they looked no bigger than pieces of birdshot. When he spoke, his words were thick and distorted with his passion.

'This is the end for you, Kirby!'

That was all. He jerked his head at Steve, heeled sharply and went out into the street. Still holding his head, Bodie followed.

Kirby breathed a heavy sigh of relief and dabbed at the beads of sweat on his forehead.

Man, if looks could kill, there'd be two funerals in Beaumont Flats day after tomorrow! One of them his!

'The hell we gonna do now, Jed?' Steve Bodie asked, feeling dizzy, his head throbbing. 'Want me to drag the men outta the bar and set 'em to lookin' for Santee?'

'He ain't in town, you damn fool!' snapped the rancher. 'He rode the night train out, that's what he done!'

'Hell, that was more'n an hour ago!'

'Don't worry – I can send a couple of telegrams and have him picked up at the first stop.' He looked savagely back towards the law office. 'But I meant it when I said

Kirby was finished! And I mean tonight!'

Bodie shook his head, wanting it clear now. 'You want me to lay for him?'

'Not like you think – Kirby's just a mite too damn popular to risk that – but there's another way...' He took some coins from his pocket and handed them to Bodie. 'Go see the boys ain't gettin' too thirsty.'

'Judas, with what you gave 'em they'll drink the bar dry!'

'An' cut loose their curly wolves – yeah, I know my crew. And they know me – they'll savvy what to do when you explain... You feel up to it?'

Bodie nodded gently. 'Yeah, Jed, I know what you mean – I'll see to it.'

Wes Santee wasn't sure just what was going through his mind. All he knew was he was stunned by Deborah's appearance from behind the water-tank support.

She was dressed for travelling in a dark-green ankle-length dress with a white lace collar and bodice showing at the vee-shaped neckline. The cuffs were also matching white lace. She wore a simple ring with an emerald for a stone and a hat of the same colour as her dress, cocked a trifle jauntily, perhaps, but which gave her a somewhat

78

demure appearance.

A young woman not too sure of herself, travelling alone...

She had two small valises, one of leather, the other made of a sort of tapestry material. Santee carried one as they made their way through the darkness beyond the railway siding and the lights of the depot buildings. She led the way, more familiar with this place than he was. Apart from her greeting – which had left him speechless – all she had said was,

'Come with me. I know where we can talk in private.'

Then she had shown him the two valises and he had automatically picked up one. He would have taken both except he had his warbag and grub sack to carry.

He followed her, trying to figure out what was going on. It was obvious she had either been on the train and left it before it pulled away from the siding, or she had been going to board it but had changed her mind.

Still, it was mighty strange that she had been lurking – hiding? – down by the water-tanks, quite a distance from the train. And the depot buildings.

They skirted the very edge of town and she took him to a small disused cabin by a clump of trees which looked out over Main Street. She opened the door, told him to wait, and he heard her fumbling around on a shelf just inside the door. In moments she had a candle burning in a rust-spotted tin holder and he saw a heavy coating of dust on the scarred deal table and chairs and the single-frame bed that had a sagging and rotted network of leather webbing dangling to the floor beneath it.

She blew dust from one of the chairs and slapped at it with a small handkerchief before sitting down. Santee dropped his warbag and the valise, closed the door and hitched a hip onto the corner of the table, thumbing back his hat.

'Why didn't you stay on the train?' he asked, recalling that Abe Kirby had said Muffy Cadell was sending Deborah out of town.

Her big eyes sought his face, alternately highlighted and hidden by the flickering shadows cast by the candle flame. 'As a matter of fact, I – I was worried about you.'

'Me?'

She nodded, taking off the hat and shaking out her hair which had been bunched up. She pushed a long hatpin with an imitation-pearl handle embossed with a cherub entwined in the tendrils of some kind of vine through the hat's crown and raised her gaze to his face.

'I wasn't always a whore, Wes. I had a pretty good upbringing and my father taught me certain things that should never change, no matter what circumstances I might find myself in. One of them was to always pay my debts.'

'Well, if you mean my tackling Bo that night you more than squared-away by calling that warning out of the Dovecot's upstairs window.'

She smiled. 'You saved yourself. All I did was draw your attention to Bo waiting by the outhouse.'

'Not the way I look at it.'

'Don't you see it doesn't matter how *you* look at it? It's how *I* look at it. And when they said you were going to be brought to trial and Muffy insisted I leave town, I knew I wouldn't be able to give evidence that would help you.'

He waved it aside. 'That's a fine touch of honour you got there, Deborah. Your pa must be a good man.'

Her face straightened as she looked back down the years. 'He was,' she said quietly. 'He was a *very* good man.'

'Was? He's dead?'

She nodded and maybe there was a glint of tears in her eyes but she quickly moved her head so that her face was in shadow. 'He drowned in a flooded river. I was in business school at the time, only fifteen. My only living kin was an uncle – Uncle Dan…'

He was quick enough to pick up the touch of bitterness, and the way she spoke her uncle's name seemed to leave her with a bad taste. 'He didn't want to care for you?'

She raised her eyes to him and her mouth formed a soundless *No!* She tossed her hair out of her face. 'No, he didn't want to be bothered with me. He had his life and he didn't want me disrupting it. So he demanded a refund of my unused school fees, sold the ranch, as he was my father's executor, and – sold me.'

Santee stood quickly, an involuntary movement. He frowned. '*Sold* you! Who to–? What–?'

'A Dodge City madam. She sold me to a place in St Louis that was so dreadful, that I ran away. Eventually, Muffy found me and took me in. She has a soft side to her, you know.'

Santee scrubbed a hand around his face. 'And I figured I'd had a run of bad luck!'

'Well, now you know my background and – *no!* Please, Wes. No more – not just now anyway. I think we should find ourselves a couple of horses and then ride up into the hills.'

'The hell've you got in mind?'

But she didn't get a chance to answer. There were the sounds of several random shots and, drifting in their wake, a string of catcalls from drunken men.

'That'll be the Flying H,' she said. 'About a third of Jed Handy's crew is in town drinking.'

'Well, I'd say they were out for trouble by the sounds of things…'

Then there were three more swift gunshots, overlaid by the roar of a shotgun and the sound of shattering glass. There were two more gunshots and the girl gasped as Santee's Colt seemed to simply appear in his hand as he lunged for the door.

'Where are you going?'

'That was Kirby's shotgun. If he tried to break up that drunken bunch, I reckon he found trouble. Stay here!'

She heard his boots pounding away into the night.

6
Beaten!

Too late, Abe Kirby realized he had been set up.

Those first gunshots and the wolf-howling and loud cussing had brought him hurrying out of his office, snapping the Greener's breech closed on two 12-gauge shells loaded with double-aught buckshot.

He made for the Drover's Palace but realized the Flying H crew must have moved on to Bink Daniels' Red River saloon. He swung that way, breaking into a sprint as glass shattered and there was a roar from a dozen booze-blurred voices.

He burst in through the batwings, saw the chaos that he had expected – Flying H making trouble, kicking over furniture, sometimes with occupants still sitting on the chairs or a man's drinks or supper on the table. Just hunting trouble...

There were scuffles, Flying H cowboys urging on their companions to turn them into a full-scale brawl.

'All right, all *right!*' bawled the sheriff, stepping into the room and brandishing the shotgun. 'That's enough! You Flyin' H men line up at the bar... Come on! *Move,* damn you!'

'Aw, leave 'em be, Kirby. They been workin' damn hard and they deserve a break.'

Steve Bodie stepped out of the shadows of a corner by the abandoned piano – apparently the regular player had seen there was going to be trouble and had run for cover. Bodie was smirking, the thumb of his right hand hooked into his gun belt an inch or so in front of his holster.

That was when Abe Kirby knew he had been set up.

Bodie was a tough *hombre* but he didn't use such menacing gestures often, preferring to hammer a man into submission with his big fists, rather than try to outdraw him. But the ramrod was mighty fast and men he had killed in shoot-outs had always been provoked into making the first move towards their guns. Yet on every occasion, the killing had been labelled 'self-defence'.

And now Kirby knew Jed Handy was ready to make his big move on the valley, had sent Bodie to arrange this and make it look like Kirby had been caught up in a drunken brawl.

Now, Kirby swung his shotgun slowly around to cover the foreman. Steve merely smiled. Without looking at the Handy crew, he said quietly, 'Turn loose the wolf, boys.'

It was the signal they were waiting for and in an instant the cowboys were turning on the townsmen nearest them slugging at them without provocation, filling the bar-room with a seething mass of fighting bodies in seconds. A couple pulled their guns and loosed off a few gunshots into the high roof of the bar-room.

Kirby stepped aside, trying to keep Bodie covered, but there were always some fighting men blocking his view. Desperately, Kirby fired the first barrel into the roof and even before the laths and paint-flakes had finished falling, he had the second hammer cocked and at last got a clear shot at Bodie.

Except Bodie fired first, three fast, hammering shots, and the sheriff staggered, flailing backwards, the shotgun thundering into the floorboards. As Kirby fell, Bodie fired again and the brawlers closed in, the Flying H men refusing to stop because of the gunfire. Others not involved in the fights ran for the doors when they saw the bloody figure of Abe Kirby on the floor being trampled underfoot.

The whole bar-room was nothing but utter chaos – the brawlers stumbling all round the place, men shouting, others scurrying for cover or the exits, all taking place under a pall of reeking powdersmoke that stung the eyes and hacked at the throat.

And this was the scene that greeted Wes Santee as he smashed his way through the batwings, shoving and kicking past men running out.

At first he didn't see Kirby because of the milling brawlers and then a man slipped in some blood and opened up a gap in the crowd. Santee stiffened when he saw the dead lawman – and he knew his hunch had been right. As soon as he had heard the gunfire and the sounds of an all-in brawl, he had figured someone had laid a trap for Abe Kirby.

And he had arrived too late to do anything about it.

Or had he?

He pushed and clubbed his way through the mass of men, having seen Bink Daniels standing at one end of the bar with his two bouncers, uncertain about making a move. The saloon owner looked warily at Santee.

'How'd it happen, Bink?'

Daniels' gaze went past Santee's shoulder and then he said, fighting to be heard above the sounds of battle, 'It was an ambush but they're makin' it look like Kirby got killed durin' the brawl. There've been wild shots for some time.'

'I heard 'em. Who did it, Bink?'

Again Daniels' gaze slipped past Santee and this time the drifter turned and saw Steve Bodie reloading his sixgun, one shoulder pushing against the wall. The challenging smirk on the brutal foreman's face told Santee all he wanted to know.

As soon as he started forward, the fighting began to ease off and by the time he was facing Bodie squarely, there were only one or two isolated punches being thrown.

Everyone was watching this confrontation with Bodie and the ramrod left no doubt as to which direction he wanted the meeting to take.

'Well, well, well. I heard you'd run outta town like a cur dog with his tail tucked up between his legs, 'breed.'

'Don't believe all you hear, Bodie.' Santee gestured to the battered, drunken Flying H crew. 'You gonna have some of them hold me again while you beat up on me?'

Steve laughed. 'Hell, no. I don't need anyone to hold you – I was just softenin' you up for Will that other time.'

'Good to know,' Santee said casually and then struck with his gun barrel, fast as a striking snake.

The metal took Bodie across the side of the head, knocking his hat halfway down the bar. The big foreman staggered and stumbled after it, going down to one knee. Santee holstered his Colt without haste, walked up to the dazed ramrod and lifted a knee savagely into the brutal face. Steve's nose crunched with a sound that was heard in every corner of the suddenly hushed room. The impact sent him sprawling along the brass footrail, one hand knocking over a spittoon.

Santee kicked him in the hard body and Bodie grunted, instinct making him roll away. But an arm caught in the footrail and held him for a second kick that took him in the chest. Strangely, it seemed to bring him back from semi-consciousness. His wild eyes flew wide and they burned with hatred as they focused on Santee. Thick arms thrust against the sawdusted floor and Bodie came surging up, taking a punch alongside the jaw but riding it smoothly, parrying the drifter's next blow and driving a meaty fist into Santee's midriff.

Wes Santee stumbled, his legs buckling slightly and Bodie waded in, following with a barrage of punches that would have floored a mustang. Santee went down but had enough sense to start rolling the moment he hit the floor. Bodie stepped after him, swinging a boot, missed, and lost balance. Santee came up as if shot from a cannon and the top of his skull cracked under Bodie's lantern jaw.

The shouting onlookers were suddenly silent.

Santee saw stars and felt his legs buckle again, but Steve Bodie's head snapped back as if his neck was broken. He staggered, big arms flailing, knocking down one cowboy who tried to steady him. Santee elbowed the cowboy aside, went after the ramrod, ran at him and carried him back across the bar. The rolled-zinc edge smashed into Bodie's spine and his whole body creaked as he arched over the counter-top, scattering glasses and bottles. He snatched at one bottle, got hold of it by the neck and swung at Santee.

The drifter dropped to one knee and Bodie missed with the blow but was quick enough to lift a knee into Santee's chest. Wes floundered, skidding along the floor. Bodie threw the bottle and it hit Santee on the shoulder, numbing his arm. The Flying H man lunged in, baring his teeth which were all bloody from his streaming, mashed nostrils. Both arms flailed and Santee tried to parry but his numbed arm refused to work. Some of the blows got through and he felt them shake him to his boots. He half-turned to dodge a fist whistling towards his face but it felt as if it had torn off his right ear, skidding along the side of his weaving head.

Stung with the pain that brought a howl bursting out of him, he swung backwards and his crooked elbow took Bodie across the bridge of his already battered nose. The man let out a yell and clapped both hands to his face instinctively. Santee immediately went downstairs, arms going like pistons as he drove blow after blow into the thick midsection, forcing Bodie back, step by step. He staggered as he tried to find his balance.

Santee kicked at his legs in an effort to knock him down. He partly succeeded but Bodie fell towards him, got an arm about his neck and crushed his face against his muscled torso. Grunting aloud he ran at the bar, intent on driving Santee face first into the edge. The drifter could just see what was happening and thrust a leg between Bodie's. They fell with a clatter, a tangle of arms and legs, and then writhing, floundering bodies rolled across the floor, splintering chairs and tables already damaged by the cowboys. Bodie snatched a shattered chair-leg and tried to drive the splintered end into Santee's eyes. The drifter wrenched his head aside, got a forearm across Bodie's throat and slammed him back against the end of the bar. His boots scrabbled for a hold as he threw his full weight on that arm. Bodie's air was cut off, his face congested and his big hands clawed frantically. Desperately, he forked two thick fingers and stabbed at Santee's eyes. Wes ducked and lost his concentration for a moment, long enough for Bodie to break the hold and scramble away on all fours.

But Santee leapt up and was waiting when Bodie roared to his feet. Brutal knuckles smashed the sound back into his teeth and Santee grabbed him by the blood-slippery ears, held him and head-butted him between the eyes. Bodie's legs sagged and Santee roared with the effort of supporting the man as he ran him for the batwings, lurched to one side and thought *To hell with it!* and flung the ramrod through a window.

Glass exploded out onto the boardwalks where men had gathered to watch. They scattered as Bodie's body caught up on the sill and hung there, bloody, immobile – beaten.

Bink Daniels grabbed the staggering Santee's arm and steadied him. 'Come into the back room – I got a bottle of good whiskey there for you.'

Santee squinted at him through a closing left eye, his right one blurred by blood from a cut on his forehead.

'Only – one?' he panted. 'Better – roll in a – keg!'

Bink smiled and nodded to one of his bouncers who took the drifter's other arm as his legs gave way. They half carried, half dragged him back to the private room behind the bar.

The stunned crowd was just beginning to come to life, animated conversation starting, men shaking their heads in disbelief, the general consensus summed up by the same words that were uttered over and over.

'I don't b'lieve it! I seen Steve Bodie fought to a standstill!'

'Just goes to show. *Anyone* can be beat, you got the right man to do it.'

Deborah saw the crowds on the boardwalks outside the Red River saloon and skirted the edge, keeping an eye out for Muffy Cadell or any of the other 'soiled doves' she had worked with. She had to make tiny jumps in the air so as to see over the heads of the jostling crowd and in the end asked Jackson, the baker, in his floury white apron, what had happened.

'Sheriff Kirby got hisself killed by Steve Bodie, for a start,' Jackson said, a wizened man but now with a twinkle of excitement in his rheumy eyes.

'For a start?' Deborah asked, feeling the anxiety rising within her.

'Yep. Then that 'breed drifter, Santee, come in and whaled the tar outta Bodie! I arrived just before the end but I wish I'd seen it from the start. He left Steve hangin' out of a busted window, cut up somethin' awful and beat black and blue. Musta been one helluva fight. Damn! I wish I'd seen it all! But this blasted bakery and folk wantin' fresh bread every day – you know I...'

'Yes, I know how hard you work, Mr Jackson, and long hours, too. But what happened to Santee?'

'The 'breed? Hell, I dunno. They say Bink

and his bouncers dragged him out back someplace. Reckon he couldn't walk...'

He looked around him, suddenly realizing she was gone, and shrugging, he pressed forward to look into the bar-room where Cropp the deputy was organizing a couple of men to transfer Kirby's body to an old door, getting ready to carry the dead lawman over to the undertaker's.

Cropp was flushed, and wished Benbow, the other deputy was here, but the man was making the most of his so-called belly-ache and staying a-bed. That way he took no risks of getting beat up or worse by the Flying H.

'I need a statement from somebody about what happened here,' Cropp said, looking around the room.

Men opened out and revealed the battered and bleeding Steve Bodie being supported by a couple of Flying H cowpokes. The ramrod glared at Cropp.

'Kirby stuck his nose in what was no more'n a friendly brawl,' Bodie said, his speech slurred because of his smashed mouth and broken teeth. 'Got caught by some high-jinks. If he'd stayed outta things and let the boys let off some steam he wouldn't've walked into them bullets.'

Cropp paled a little, feeling sick as he faced

Steve Bodie. 'Someone said *you* shot him.'

'Then "someone" don't know what they're talkin' about. Hell, I mighta got off a couple shots like the rest of the boys, but if they ricocheted and nailed Kirby, you can hardly pin this on me.'

The Flying H crew backed him up, all putting hard stares on Cropp, making him irresolute.

'Well, I gotta have some sorta statement – for the records... Hell, I dunno who's gonna be sheriff now, but I need to have the books up to date.'

Bodie suddenly pulled free of the cowboys, staggered, holding a blood-soaked kerchief to a deep cut on his face. He swayed as he looked down at Kirby's body on the door being held patiently by two townsmen, awaiting an order to go.

Bodie reached out and jerked the blood-spattered star from Kirby's shirt. Men gasped and stared incredulously as Bodie pinned the star on his own torn shirt and grinned, one tooth still hanging by a shred of flesh in his gums.

'Reckon if the position's vacant, I might as well take it. Won't be fit to do no range work for a spell, but reckon I can handle a patrol around this here town and a little paper-work. Or maybe you can handle the paper-work, eh, Cropp?'

The deputy was grey-faced now, licked his lips, wanting to protest, but even his youthful recklessness wouldn't allow him to bluster and tell Bodie he couldn't just take Kirby's badge like that.

He cleared his throat. 'Well – I...'

'Don't worry about it, Cropp,' Bodie slurred as the young deputy stammered, looking for words that wouldn't come. 'I might not want a deputy, anyway. We'll see. You might's well go home for the night. I'll see to things here.'

'Listen, Steve, I dunno about this...'

'You're right there, Cropp – you're only a deputy and too young. So you go on home like I said – I'll send for you if I need you.' Bodie almost smiled, adding, 'If I don't send for you, means I don't need you – I'll likely appoint my own deputy. *Buenos noches,* Cropp, ol' *amigo.*'

Cropp looked hangdog, flushing, thought for a wild moment of going for his gun, but when he saw the menacing Handy crew and Bodie just waiting for him to do something stupid like that, he swallowed audibly, heeled sharply and stomped out.

The laughter from the Flying H crew rang

in his ears all the way home.

Bink Daniels' wife and young daughter patched up Santee in the back room. The saloon man helped him keep the pain at bay with regular medicinal doses of bonded bourbon that he kept only for very special occasions.

But he paused once, and lifted his own shotglass mouth-high, saying, 'To Abe Kirby. A good man, but no match for the sons of bitches runnin' this valley!'

His wife snapped at him for using such language in front of their fourteen-year-old daughter but the girl smiled, slyly: she had heard worse, had *said* worse, with her friends in Ballinger's barn behind the haystack while they smoked cigarettes and explored the difference between boys and girls...

'I'll drink to that.' Santee's voice was slurred, but not only from his swollen mouth and the cut inner cheeks. Bink's whiskey was reaching up into his brain and he was beginning to feel very relaxed and pleased with himself.

'That really the first time anyone's ever beat Bodie?' he asked Daniels for the third or fourth time and Mrs Daniels shook her head slowly, sighing.

'First time, Wes. Refill?'

'Think I better not, Bink,' Wes Santee slurred. 'Reckon I best get outta town for a spell – if you can lend me a bronc...'

'Sure, that's not–'

'I already have horses.'

They all turned sharply as Deborah Hatfield entered by the rear door, flushed. Santee noticed she had changed out of the green frock and lacy blouse into a checked shirt, corduroy trousers and tooled-leather riding boots. She wore a short-waisted corduroy jacket over the shirt and a hat with a narrow brim, held in place by a leather thong under her chin, kept firm by a carved deerhorn slide. A short, plaited quirt dangled from her right wrist.

Mrs Daniels and the young girl stared somewhat rudely at Deborah but before the woman could speak, Santee said,

'Where'd you get horses?'

Deborah looked at him sharply, hearing the slur in his words. 'Well, the Flying H crew seem intent on drinking your bar dry, Bink, and they left their horses at the hitch rail outside the Drover's Palace, and I thought, Jed Handy's no doubt behind all this trouble tonight; so...'

She paused and shrugged. 'Are you up to

riding, Wes?' she asked the drifter and he nodded, the movement just a mite out of control. 'You're – sure? We have a long way to go.'

Her words somehow reached through the blur that was taking him over and he frowned, squinted. 'Long way–? To where?'

She took his arm, seeing how battered he was and wondering just what Steve Bodie looked like. 'Come on, I'll explain when we clear town.' She glanced around at the others a little apologetically. 'If you don't know where we're going, you can't tell anyone. I hope you understand, Bink.'

Bink said he did but Mrs Daniels' disapproving, tight-lipped face said she was offended. The woman held open the door, looking hostile and impatient.

'I hope you know what you're doing, young I – I was about to say "young lady", but I don't think that's quite appropriate here.'

Deborah gave her a dazzling smile. 'I'm young, anyway. Come on, Wes. We really do have a long ride ahead of us.'

Santee moved stiffly, groaning a little, limping.

'Hell – and I was the *winner!*' he moaned as Deborah led him out into the night.

101

7
Outlaw Country

By the time they had cleared Beaumont Flats, the noise behind them in the street telling them that the Flying H hadn't yet finished painting the town red, the fresh air had cleared Santee's head some.

He was mighty stiff and sore and knew he would feel worse tomorrow. The girl seemed sure of where they were going and when they reached a creek and he could sense rather than see broken country ahead, he asked,

'Where are we bound?'

'Heading into what used to be known as outlaw country.'

'*Used* to be?'

'Things changed once the railroad drove through and a few towns sprang up. But there are still outlaws who have their hideouts in the same area.'

'And we're going to join a bunch of outlaws, I suppose.'

She turned and he saw the pale blur of her

face and the flash of her teeth as she smiled. 'Exactly.'

She spurred away and Santee was a little slow off the mark but he caught up with her within about twenty yards, leaned from the saddle and grabbed her mount's bridle, slowing and finally halting both horses.

'Time to talk.'

'We can't spare the time! Do you think Jed Handy will just let you go? You killed Will, no matter how justifiable, and he won't rest until you're dead. You may have beaten Steve Bodie in a fight, but neither of them fights fair. They'll both use every trick they know to track you down and kill you, Wes!'

Her earnestness reached him. 'Then it's time we split up.'

'No! You don't know this country. They would have you cornered in no time at all.'

He frowned though he knew she couldn't see his face in this light. 'How come *you* know this neck of the woods? I had you figured for a town gal.'

He heard the smile in her voice. 'I told you I was raised on a ranch. I like the outdoors...'

She paused, looking at him sidelong as if waiting for some comment. He started to make one but remained silent. Then she continued.

'Jed Handy has been riding roughshod over everyone in the valley for a long time. He's bought up some land he lost because of the railroad coming through, but in other cases, he's forced people off – or forced them to sell to him for ridiculously low prices.'

'Sounds like standard range-grabbing. I've fought in more than one range war.'

'Well, most of those people who were forced to quit the valley moved on somewhere else. But a few couldn't afford to or were too stubborn to, and they stayed. Not in Beaumont Valley, of course, but within a couple of days' ride or closer.'

'Uh-huh. The fighters, eh? The ones who were beat by Handy but refused to give up.'

'Ye-es – I suppose that's how it is.'

'And you're taking me to such a bunch?'

'Yes. I know this group. There are only four; led by a man called Todd Rainey. He lost a few hundred acres of good river-bottom land, refused to sell to Handy no matter what he had Bodie do, and eventually Jed just rode in and literally drove him off with bullets buzzing around him.'

Santee remained silent. He had seen this happen before: stubborn men, not necessarily courageous, but goddamned *stubborn!*

Pig-headed, more like. Didn't know when to call it quits and get out while they still had a whole skin. Not that Santee himself was a quitter – he had fought for land, *his* land, once, a long time ago. It had gotten his wife and kids killed...

He would bend the knee to no man but what haunted him most, what drove him on an endless, ultimately pointless quest for – *something* – was the knowledge that if he had listened to his wife a little earlier, said to hell with the land – *'It's only a piece of dirt, Wes, that's all, when you get right down to it – and if you'll realize that, and let them have it, we can find another piece of land somewhere else, where we can be happy and watch our family grow...'*

Of course, he hadn't listened to her and while he was away, tracking the last of his cattle that had been stolen, someone had set fire to the ranch house – after nailing all the doors shut...

He shook himself now. 'I've no notion to fight another man's battles for him, Deborah.'

'Well, Todd Rainey talks a good fight so they say, but I think I've read you right, Wes Santee. You've been wronged by Jed Handy and Steve Bodie, and you feel bad about Abe Kirby's death, even though you had

106

nothing to do with it and couldn't have saved him even if you had been there – and I think you're the kind of man who won't ride on until you've squared things.'

He half smiled although it hurt. '"Squared" things – you talk more country than town, now and again.'

'Let's get on, Wes,' she said with urgency in her voice. 'It's a long way and we may have to camp until it's daylight so I can find some of the landmarks.'

She became lost – or unsure of direction – a couple of hours later and they made cold camp in a dry wash. No one could come up on them from the end of the wash which was so badly eroded some of the gutters were deeper than Santee was tall. The entrance was narrow and the sides high and crumbly; anyone fool enough to try to approach by the sides would find the desiccated soil sliding away beneath their feet.

'It's not the first time you've been a – fugitive,' the girl remarked.

'No,' he said and didn't elaborate.

After they had shared a canteen she saw him looking at her. There was some starlight and she couldn't see his features, but she sensed he was staring hard at her.

'What's wrong?'

'Just wondering – about you.'

She laughed briefly and there was a note of relief in the sound. 'Why am I a whore?'

'I guess it's none of my business,' he said curtly.

'Probably not. But – I told you about my uncle not wanting me. Well, he didn't want the trouble of keeping me and looking after me but – he did *want* me – in one way...'

She paused and Santee nodded. 'I savvy what you mean.'

'Yes. After he'd sold the ranch and stolen all the money he could from me, he sold me to a woman who ran a bunch of "soiled doves", working out of a couple of covered wagons. I don't know if it was conscience or not, but he gave me two double eagles, said it was for being *nice* to him one certain night – not that I'd had any choice. He said it was more than the "going rate" but I was worth it. I would make any man – happy.' She paused again and when she continued he heard the slight edge to her words. 'So – I thought, well, it's a lot more than I could earn as a bookkeeper ... so why not learn a trade that pays well?'

He remained silent for a time, spoke

quietly when he did say something. 'Hard way to make money, though, isn't it?'

She liked that: none of the usual censure, at least not in the form of a lecture, quoting from the Bible and so on... 'I want a lot of money.'

He frowned at the determination in her voice. 'Most folk can get by on a lot less than they figure they need.'

'I don't know how much I need, but it will be a lot more than I have.'

'You mind if I ask – why?'

'It's simple: I want to take my uncle to court and prove he stole my inheritance, and that means hiring the best lawyer in the land.'

After a while he started to settle on his thin blankets, tilted his hat over his battered face and said quietly into the night,

'I wish you luck.'

Come morning and they started to climb into the Chevron Hills.

Santee was surprised how well the girl seemed to know them, leading the way along narrow trails that clung to sheer walls like a piece of string stuck to the side of a box. The horses were not happy and snorted and danced – until her grey kicked away the edge of the trail and sent a few pounds of rock plummeting into space. They settled a bit after that – temporarily at least. Luckily, they were trained cow ponies, used to dangerous country. They might not like it but old habits die hard and they grudgingly obeyed the signals of reins and spurs.

Not that there was much spurring done on the narrow trail which Deborah said was known as 'Safeway'.

'Somebody has a peculiar sense of humour,' she added, half-hipping in the saddle to look at Santee.

He sat awkwardly because of his stiffness and sore parts of his anatomy which didn't allow full flexibility of his battered body.

'You'll be all right?' she asked, her face reflecting her concern. 'It's not too far now.'

'I'm OK. But how in hell did you know the way up here?'

'Oh, I've been here before,' she said off-handedly.

'Into outlaw country, along secret trails? A mite off the beaten track for you, ain't it?'

She smiled. 'I don't suppose you meant that to come out as a pun – but, yes, it is. But Muffy sent me out here with another girl from the Dovecot, last year.'

'Well, how the hell did she know about it?'

'Oh, didn't I mention that Todd Rainey is her brother-in-law? No? Well, he is. Her husband actually had a share in the river-bottom land with him but he was killed in a stampede and Todd was trying to manage things when Jed Handy ran him off. Todd's a little – weak, I guess is the word.'

Santee shook his head slowly. 'Why did Muffy send you to him?' Immediately he had asked the question he saw the answer and felt his bruised face burning with embarrassment. 'Listen, forget I asked – I didn't mean to–'

'It's OK,' she said brightly. 'It was his birthday and Muffy said he was depressed and needed something to cheer him up. His men, too.' She spread her hands, but quickly grabbed at the reins again. 'So – she sent Della and me as – gifts.'

He sighed. 'Look, Deborah, I ain't no prude, but – well, whoring just don't seem – right – for you somehow.'

She smiled. 'You're nice, Wes. But don't concern yourself. I'm told that most people don't really enjoy their work. And that's all it is to me. A job. So I can earn money – a lot faster than if I was pushing a pen in some dreary office.'

Santee decided to drop it. She had more

strength of character than he would have expected in a young woman of her background, and she had a purpose and had set her sights and aimed to hit her target when she was ready.

It was no business of his how she did it.

It was midday before they found the outlaws' hideaway.

The camp was in a broken canyon, stream-fed and grassy, and it held a few cattle, a rough corral containing half a dozen horses. Behind was a ramshackle cabin with a patched roof – a weathered tarp strung over an area of missing shingles. The windows were boarded, only one appearing to be hinged, and the door was askew and wouldn't close properly.

Some lazy types live here, thought Santee as the girl led the way in. One by one three men appeared from the rocks within the vicinity of the cabin, and a fourth came out of the cabin itself. They all held rifles. The man from the cabin shaded his eyes and then called out.

'That you Deborah Hatfield?'

'It's me, Todd! This is my friend, Wes Santee.'

'Looks like a damn 'breed!'

112

She snapped her head around and Santee said quietly, 'Well, that's a good beginning.'

'Oh, don't mind Todd. He feels guilty that he gave in to Jed Handy. He means well.'

'Don't sound like it to me.'

But when they dismounted and she handled the introductions, Todd Rainey gripped firmly enough with Santee and looked him straight in the eye.

'That bit about the 'breed just kinda slipped out.' It was near enough to an apology and Santee smiled faintly.

'Happens you're right – Grandmother was a full-blood Choctaw.'

Rainey's smile grew a mite smaller but he nodded before he introduced his three companions: Windy, Bourbon, and Corey Skinner. The latter was not much larger than a youth in his teens but he must have been pushing forty-five pretty damn hard, Santee reckoned. He wore a patch over one eye and the same side of his face was puckered with a bad scar. He didn't speak as he gripped hands, merely stared hard with his single eye. Windy was a bearded, frog-faced, but cheerful-looking cuss somewhere in his thirties – his body was, leastways. Later Santee was to find out that his mind was lost somewhere back in his teen years.

Bourbon had a nose to go with his name, dark red, shot through with a mud-map of vari-coloured veins, the nostrils pinched and moist. He reeked of stale booze and sweat and had a handshake like a limp, wet fish.

Not an impressive group.

Todd Rainey himself was in his late twenties and he had eyes mostly for Deborah, sidled up to her and slid his arm about her slim waist, letting the hand wander. Until she stomped her riding-boot heel on his instep and pushed him away roughly.

'It's not your birthday, Todd!'

He shrugged. 'Well, I got some money...'

Her eyes narrowed. 'This visit is for business, not pleasure.' She explained quickly and Rainey's hatchet-face sobered, his beer-coloured eyes looking at Santee with new respect.

Windy whistled between his yellowed teeth. 'He acshly knocked out Bodie...?' He couldn't believe it, you could tell by his voice. 'Wish I coulda seen that! Wow-eeee!'

Deborah assured him it was true and Bourbon sniffed, asked for a description of the fight. Santee said 'Later', he was too tired now and needed some grub.

They led the way into the cabin and it

stank of unwashed clothes and stale food. Deborah started laying down the law, had them scrubbing grease-caked skillets and pans with coarse sand and lye soap in no time at all. She pushed a pail of hot water and lye into Windy's hands and a worn scrubbing-brush and ordered him to scrub the table.

'You can leave any time you want!' he muttered but set about the chores.

'I'm not sleeping in any of those bunks,' the girl declared and Rainey winked, grinning.

'You wouldn't be sleepin' if you climbed into mine, even if it was brand-new and shinin' like a new penny!'

She shot a cold look toward him. 'I told you, Todd, this is a business visit. You have any other ideas, forget them.' She said the last as she reached into one of her draw-string bags and brought out a Remington-Elliott four-barrelled derringer with a ring trigger. She showed it around.

No one was grinning after that. They went about their chores with angry, violent movements, Rainey shooting hostile looks at Santee.

But they thawed by the time Deborah had cooked up a decent meal with the fresh grub and vegetables she had brought and Santee handed around his tobacco sack: there was precious little left when he got it back, but he didn't mind.

'So, what's the plan, Santee?' Rainey asked, smoking the thick cigarette he had rolled.

'Will Handy's being buried tomorrow. Jed's bullied the whole valley and town into going to the funeral,' Santee said quietly. 'Seems to me we ought to be able to cash in on that – I mean, it leaves his ranch unattended, or with maybe just the cook and a couple of token guards. We could go into the cattle business...'

Windy, Bourbon and Skinner seemed interested but Rainey merely stared, squinting against the upcurling smoke from his cigarette. He shook his head.

'Hard to hide cattle tracks getting in here. Takes a long time because of the way the country is,' he said slowly, eyes never leaving Santee's face. 'Handy's men could track us down before we could get away and we'd have to just leave the damn cows for 'em to collect.'

'Sounds like it's happened before,' Santee allowed and Rainey's mouth tightened, then Windy said,

116

'It has – twice. Used to be six of us, but Bodie an' his crew killed Ben Turrow and Mad Chad Pinney.'

'Shut up, Windy!' growled Rainey, drawing hard on his smoke.

'Well, what d'you do here?' Santee wanted to know. He looked around at the four outlaws. 'You harry Handy as much as you can? How d'you live?'

'We do jobs when we need money,' Rainey told him curtly. 'You don't need to know the details. As for rilin' Handy, why we run off some of his herds when we can get close enough, stampede 'em, or fire a pasture now and then...'

Santee nodded knowingly and Rainey broke off frowning. 'The hell would you know about it, anyway?' Rainey demanded. 'Ain't none of your business!'

'I fought a range-grabber once. He'd killed my family and I was damned if I was gonna move on without seeing him destroyed. I eventually did it and killed him. But I *worked* at it. I didn't sit around, waiting for a sunny day or a wet night before I gave him plenty of aggravation.'

'You sayin' that's what we do?' Rainey was getting mad.

'Way it sounds.'

'Yeah, and it's the way it is!' Skinner said. 'See this face of mine? Bodie did that to me on Jed's orders. Marked me with his spurs, but the rowel slipped and took my eye with it! I wanted to do plenty more'n what we have done but Rainey figures he's the leader and–'

'I *am* the leader!' Todd Rainey said, rearing to his feet, the movement holding a hint of challenge in it. 'And you better remember that, Santee! You got any ideas, you pass 'em along to me first and I'll be the one to say what we do about 'em.'

'If that works for you and others, fine. But I'll do things my way and I'll stay outta your hair.'

'Damn right you will!' Todd Rainey growled. 'You don't do things the way I want 'em, you don't stay here at all, mister!'

'Fine with me. Just let me rest up tonight and I'll be on my way tomorrow. These hills must have better hideouts than this. And men who have bigger scores to settle with Jed Handy than you lot. Men who'll *do* something about it.'

Deborah had sat silent, watching the men; now she said quietly in the brief hush that followed Santee's words,

'I might be only a whore, but I have a

brain and I agree with Wes that we have to take advantage of Handy emptying the town for Will's funeral.' She turned to Santee. 'Why don't you tell them that idea you had on the way up here, Wes? I think it'll work...'

'So that's the way the wind's blowin'!' muttered Rainey but no one paid him any heed. They were all looking expectantly at Santee now.

He nodded. 'Gents, what I have in mind will not only hit Jed Handy where he lives, but we stand a good chance of coming out of this with a lot of money. Anyone interested?'

8
Red River Funeral

It was the biggest – and possibly the best – funeral north Texas had ever seen or was ever likely to see.

It was on a grand scale when you compared it to the usual settlers' ceremony held in the churchyard or at a graveside in Boot Hill at the western edge of town. Will Handy might not have been popular in Beaumont Flats when he was alive but a stranger arriving would never have got that impression.

There were crowds. Crowds everywhere. Too many to fit into the Episcopalian church and so they overflowed onto the weed-cluttered lawn and path outside while the nervous preacher went through the usual routine. His nervousness was caused by one of Jed Handy's men standing beside the pulpit, his hair slicked down with water, wearing his best shirt buttoned to the throat, worn and faded, though tolerably clean Levis, and scuffed riding-boots that had been brushed and coated with neat-foot oil. There was also the gun-rig he wore and while he leaned back against one end of the organ, arms folded, his eyes were hard, scanning the crowd, and often – too often, maybe – seeking out the preacher as the man's voice shook a little while reciting the funeral service.

There were other Flying H cowboys scattered around the walls and amongst the crowd outside.

Will's elaborate highly polished coffin was closed, silver handles and nameplate gleaming in the dusty sunlight that streamed through the church's narrow windows. At a shaky sign from the preacher, six of the men became pall-bearers, led by grim-faced Steve Bodie, some of whose injuries had been partly covered with creams and a dusting of powder. So Will was transferred to the newly varnished hearse with its glass-panelled sides, sliding in soundlessly, and the wildflowers Jed had demanded the townsfolk collect and make into wreaths, were piled in to cover the casket.

The undertaker was sick to his stomach lest something go wrong: it was many years since the hearse had been used and he wasn't too sure about the safety of the dried-out leather straps used for springing.

If they should snap… Well, it didn't bear thinking about!

Jed employed thirty men and they hurried the crowds out of town in buckboards and wagons and sulkies and even a fringed-top surrey, got them out to line the road to Will Handy's last resting place. This was on a knoll called Kate's Rest where Mrs Katherine Handy and the other two sons, Jackson and Jedediah, were buried in a small graveyard fenced with ornate iron that had been painted hurriedly only yesterday and wasn't yet quite dry. It was at the entrance to the Flying H, a mile from the ranch house, and the late Mrs Handy had liked to sit up there beneath a cottonwood tree, on a wooden platform specially built to take her rocking chair, looking out over the lush valley and creek that fed the river and pastures, listening to the birds and watching the activity in the ranchyard. When she had died several years ago from an unidentified fever, Jed had had the small graveyard built. It was for the exclusive use of the Handy family but now, with Will and the other boys dead, and no grandchildren, much of the remaining space would be wasted. For Jed would only require the usual six feet by six feet plot alongside his family. There would be no more Handys after his death.

His men saw that the crowd lined up in suitable attitudes of respect, jostling here and there, hooking an unobserved blow into the kidneys of some townsman who didn't meet their requirements. The preacher was more relaxed and in control as he read the graveside service and Will was lowered into the ground.

Dry-eyed and hard-faced, Jed Handy, in his best go-to-meeting clothes, stooped and scooped up a handful of Flying H land and sprinkled it on the lid of the descending coffin.

'Rest easy, son,' he said softly, unable to keep the catch from his voice entirely. 'The man who killed you will pay for this. *You will be avenged!*'

Then he stepped back and nodded to Bodie, who tossed in a handful of soil and started the townsfolk moving past the grave. Jed Handy stood beneath the tree that had sheltered his wife and afforded her many hours of pleasure, gravely shaking hands with the people of Beaumont Flats as they filed by, saying,

'Thanks for comin'... Thanks for payin' your respects to Will... Good of you to come...'

Just as if it wasn't all a sham...

But there wasn't a man or woman from town who was stupid enough to say so out loud.

And if they thought that was it, that it was all over once some of the Flying H hands had started filling in the grave, they were wrong, way wrong.

'The wake will be held at the ranch house,' Jed announced, startling the folk who were already preparing to move back to town, causing heads to snap around in astonishment. 'I've had a couple of bullocks killed, and two hogs. My cooks've been workin' overtime and you'll find plenty to eat. There'll be some home-made cider to drink and lemonade and maybe a tot of bottled lightnin' for them who want it. Later, when it gets dark, there'll be an hour's dancin', because my boy liked to dance and see the ladies skirts all a'swirl... So you ladies limber up and you gents unkink them muscles, because them high-jinks are about to begin!'

The townsfolk couldn't believe it. A couple of men protested and they were led away behind the barn and when they came back, both holding kerchiefs to suddenly bleeding noses, they maintained they were ready for the wingding, so let 'er rip!

No one else tried to slip away or complain.

It was a good wake, fairly noisy, but more subdued than a genuine one with folk *really* wanting to see off a well-liked friend into the next life. The cider and whiskey lowered inhibitions to a certain extent but while everyone had plenty to eat and the fiddler scratched out tune after tune for dancing, it was a stilted affair.

Jed Handy listened to it from the house. It was dark now and he could do no more. He had given Will the kind of funeral the boy would have enjoyed, even though he had had to bully everyone so that they attended.

But he had done his duty and he was exhausted from holding in his grief. Now he sat at the window in Will's darkened room, clutching a tintype of the boy which had been taken a year or so ago at some rodeo in Wichita.

There was just enough light for him to make out Will's features, the boy grinning fixedly at the camera.

And then the great grief he had tried to stifle overwhelmed Jed Handy and he clutched the tintype to his heaving chest as the tears squeezed out of those brittle old eyes and trickled and snaked down his leathery face, following the course of the wrinkles in the skin.

'Aw, boy, I had such plans for you! For you an' your family – and me. All of us together. Now there's just me – just – me. An', Will, I've never felt so downright *lonesome...*' He groaned softly as real pain gripped him.

He leaned his head forward on his arms, resting on the window sill, gasping as he held the tintype against him so that it quivered with the erratic beating of his heart.

Well, it might have been the biggest and best funeral along the Red River and the day would be long-remembered. But maybe not altogether for Will Handy's funeral.

There was another reason north Texas folk would always recall that day in July.

It was the one and only time the Red River Trust was ever robbed.

It was Deborah who gave Santee the idea. She had told him during the ride up to the hideout in outlaw country about Jed Handy hoping to take over the bank and so get control of the valley and its people.

'Sounds like there must be a lot of money in that bank's safe,' he had commented.

Later, thinking about it, and the way the town was going to be deserted because Handy's men had frightened and bullied the townsfolk until they all agreed to attend Will's funeral, Santee got to thinking that it would be a good time to pay a visit to the bank.

He told the outlaws and Todd Rainey had scowled. 'You're plumb loco! You couldn't get that safe open unless you had a key.'

'Or a few sticks of dynamite placed in the right position,' Santee had said and they all looked hard at him. 'It's been a long time, but I think I can still remember how to do it.'

'You've robbed banks before?' Rainey asked, frowning. Santee nodded curtly. 'That mean you're on the dodge with a bounty on your head?'

'No. I served my time.'

Rainey laughed. 'I ain't surprised! Robbin' banks is only for professionals!'

'That why you'd never try it, Todd?' asked Corey Skinner tightly, glancing at Santee and the girl. 'We'd starve if we didn't shoot or trap our own food. Hell, we're s'posed to be outlaws and if we can, make our livin' from Jed Handy who put us here in the first place – but Todd here won't steal cows

128

because it's too hard gettin' 'em up here and then findin' a market. Won't hold up a stage or a train because we're amateurs and likely to get shot up. Hell, wouldn't even *consider* a bank!'

He glared at Rainey who was white-faced, fists clenched. Windy sniffed and waited for Bourbon to agree with Skinner, then belatedly gave his support.

'Hell, we're *bored* here!' Skinner said, accusing Rainey to his face. 'Santee, you want to try hittin' the Red River Trust, why I'll ride with you.'

'Count me in, too,' Bourbon said, and Windy hurriedly nodded.

'If you fellers're gonna be in it, I am, too.'

Rainey jumped to his feet. 'Now, just a goddamn minute! *I'm* runnin' this gang!'

'You're idea of "running" things round here is to get as much sleep as you can, night *and* day,' growled Skinner. 'Todd, I told you we had to do somethin' or I was pullin' out. Well, Santee here's got the right idea and I'll follow him, and so will the others. So looks like you're out-voted, Todd, old pard.'

Rainey spun towards the silent girl, pointed a shaking finger at her. '*You* done this by bringin' him here! You had no right to do it, an' now look what you done! You've busted up our gang!'

'Seems it was already busted before we got here,' Santee observed mildly and it was all that Rainey needed to make him explode.

'No goddamn 'breed's takin' over my gang!' he said and snatched at his sixgun.

Santee was sitting on a rock and he rolled off, spinning and twisting so that he came to rest on one knee facing Rainey, his Colt in his hand as the other man's gun was still clearing leather.

Santee fired and Rainey howled as the lead burned across his right forearm, kicking the limb outwards, the gun tumbling to the ground. He sucked in a sharp breath and clutched the bleeding arm across his body, bent forward, teeth bared as he gritted them in pain. The others stared silently, Windy and Skinner with mouths agape.

'My God!' breathed Bourbon, blinking.

'He could have killed you, Todd,' Deborah said quietly, watching Santee.

'No need for that,' the drifter said, holstering the smoking gun. 'Rainey had a right to be riled. I got no ambitions to take over your gang, Rainey, but we need to work together to blow that bank safe. You gonna join us or

130

stay here and sulk?'

Todd Rainey allowed the girl to cut his blood-soaked sleeve and to wash the wound and wrap a bandage around it before grunting sourly,

'I'll come.'

Santee wasn't surprised. Rainey had lots of hate in him for Handy and Bodie, but not much leadership. In fact, this was a gang whose members barely tolerated each other, were only held together by their hatred for the Flying H. And it wouldn't take much to break them into individuals, for not one of them had any real loyalty to the others or the group in general.

Now his soul-chilling eyes sought Rainey and the man stiffened when he saw the look on Santee's face.

'You come, you do like you're told, savvy?'

Rainey shrugged: *Hell with that 'breed. Let him lead the others on this deal. But Rainey would be back in the saddle again, right out in front, soon after. Damn right he would!*

They started out before daylight, Rainey leading this time. And when they were in sight of the town, the first of the 'mourners' were filing into the church for the service prior to the long funeral procession going to the Flying H.

They holed up on a wooded slope in the foothills of the Chevrons, lounging about, waiting for the town to clear. Deborah sat on a log beside Santee who was just lighting a cigarette.

'I'm sorry to hear about your family, Wes.'

'Long time ago.'

'I suppose that's what set you ... drifting?'

'After I killed the range-grabber and those of his men who murdered my family.'

She remained silent for a time. 'You never tried to ... settle down again?'

He slid his gaze towards her, shook his head. 'Never seen the sense in owning property after that. Had no family, didn't want another woman, sure didn't care about owning any more land, just to have to fight to hold it. I'd likely do it different, but I'd rather not have to do it at all.'

She started to speak but caught herself in time. She thought she understood: somehow he had convinced himself he hadn't fought hard enough to hold onto his land and because of that he had lost everything; land, ranch, wife and children.

So he took to drifting, joined the restless breed, no home, no one to call family, no one to turn to for comfort or help. Just himself to rely on.

Yes, she could see all of that in Wes Santee.

But Jed Handy, another range-grabber, had stirred the old memories and passions and now Santee was out to destroy him, before moving on, saddle-tramping his way across the West. He was the kind of drifter men called 'outrider' who would bend the knee to no man, give value for money, ride for the brand when there was a brand to ride for, refuse to be pushed around, draw a line and, when someone crossed it, fight with gun or fists – *every* time.

For Santee's kind of man, there was no other way.

Maybe 'admiration' was too strong a word for what she felt about him, but she felt *something*, and it was a long time since Deborah Hatfield had had any genuine feelings for any man.

It kind of surprised her to realize it, but she knew that Santee was *her* kind of man.

9
Withdrawal

The general store presented no real problem for them. The rear door was unlocked so no actual 'breaking' was necessary. But there was a heavy padlock on the double-walled section that held the dynamite, detonators and fuses. Windy fetched a crowbar – instead of the pry bar that was requested – far too much tool for the job, but Santee gave him a nod and a wink and the man grinned in pleasure.

One tearing wrench and the lock was off. The door swung open and Santee's hunting knife blade prised up the lid of the first box marked DYNAMITE. He figured half a dozen sticks would do, crammed them into an empty flour sack handed to him by Deborah, Corey Skinner taking fuses and cartons of bright copper detonators.

The surly Todd Rainey grabbed a flour sack and after the others had gone shoved more than a dozen sticks of dynamite, two coils of fuse and two packs of detonators into it.

He also took coffee, bacon and beans, enlisting Windy's help. Santee came back to see what was causing the delay.

'We didn't come here to rob townsmen, Rainey. We only take what we need. Now leave those things and get down to the bank. Windy, bring me a hammer and cold chisel and a couple of big screwdrivers, OK?'

Windy nodded and went to look for the items. Rainey shouldered his bags and glared at Santee.

'You worry about the bank, 'breed. I'll take what I want an' the hell with you!'

He made his way out and Santee said nothing: it wasn't worth forcing the issue right now. He pointed out the tools he wanted to Windy and joined the others. They hitched the horses behind the bank building and left Windy to guard them.

Santee had to use the long crowbar to open the door, bending the security bars far enough for Skinner to get his hand through and slide back the bolts. It made a lot of noise in the quiet town but they were the only ones to hear and they filed into the bank building. Deborah showed him the safe and Santree whistled softly between his teeth. He hadn't expected such a large one for a bank servicing a town the size of Beaumont Flats, but then he realized that it serviced the whole of Red River County and over the line as well.

Bourbon rubbed his hands together, bright-eyed and eager: he had found a half-full flask of whiskey in the store and its odour was strong on his breath. 'We're gonna be rich!' he said, no doubt thinking about how much booze he would be able to buy.

'That safe's gonna take some blowing,' Skinner said, examining the edges of the door.

Santee took up the cold chisel and heavy hammer and started chipping away at the ornate pin hinges; the lock was too cumbersome for them to tackle. But exposed hinges like this gave them a good chance of success. He showed Skinner how to open up the seams where the door met the body of the safe above and below the hinge flange. He planned to lay dynamite in these grooves and hope the blast would be enough to dislodge the door.

It was crude but worked with most safes in the West at that time, although Wells Fargo always seemed to have safety devices built in on their English Chubbs.

But this was an ornate Dutch safe, thick walled, but pretty damn basic in general construction. For good measure Santee sent Bourbon back to the store for files and had him work on the large keyhole: he would jam a stick of dynamite in there, too. It was going to be a big *bang!* but there was no point in trying to muffle the noise in a deserted town.

It took longer than Santee expected but in just under an hour they had the door rigged for blasting and he bunched the fuse ends together, scratched a vesta into flame and ordered the others outside.

'Give Windy a hand with the horses. They're going to spook when this lot goes off.'

Then he set the fuses sputtering and hurried out through the rear door to where the others were waiting behind a storeroom and the outhouse.

The explosion made the ground tremble; Deborah gave a small cry of alarm, grabbing at Santee for support.

The wall of the bank also trembled. Then the windows blew out in silver showers of shattered glass, flying around dangerously close to where the bank robbers sheltered, frightening the skittish mounts even more. The rear door shot across the yard, disintegrating finally against a corner of the storeroom. Brick dust choked them in a stifling yellow cloud. Shingles slid off the edge of the jarred roof and clattered into the yard one after the other. Something inside tumbled with one hell of a crash and Santee wondered – and was proved correct shortly afterwards – if it was the safe door.

Smoke billowed out of all the new ventilation holes in the rear of the bank and Windy jumped up and did a crazy kind of dance, gobbling like a turkey and howling like a sick coyote. Rainey pulled him back angrily and flung him against the storeroom wall, telling him to shut up. Their ears rang.

They were all standing now, Bourbon and the chastised Windy soothing the settling horses. Deborah wiped dirt from her face and Santee grinned through his own mask of dust.

'And it ain't even the Fourth of July!'

She smiled and Todd Rainey scowled, starting forward. The drifter, Deborah and Skinner followed. They coughed in the smoke and dust, having to grope their way over shattered furniture, a collapsed lintel, and papers still drifting down. The heavy safe-door rested drunkenly against the wall opposite the safe itself. The big iron box seemed amazingly intact inside: all the blast had been absorbed by the heavy door-metal or blown outward.

Shelves were still in place, some papers curled and charred but mostly intact. Record books had been dislodged but seemed unharmed.

But the main thing they noticed was that there was very little money. Just a few small piles of bills and two canvas bags of coins with the bank's name stencilled on them. Rainey shouldered the girl aside rudely and reached in, scooping up some of the stacked bills. He flicked through them quickly.

'These are only fives! Ain't more'n a couple hundred in each stack!'

Deborah took up some of the others, flicking the edges to see their denomination. 'There are some twenties and tens, and one pile of fifties,' she said slowly, frowning as she turned. 'Banker Aimes is a very smart and zealous man, Wes – I imagine he shipped any large amounts of cash before today, knowing the town would be deserted and therefore open to robbery if anyone was so inclined.'

'How much is there?' snapped Rainey, still stuffing bundles of bills into a coffee sack he had brought along specially for this purpose.

'I'd say roughly – five thousand, including

the coins. This bank could operate on that amount of cash on a daily basis fairly easily, I imagine.'

Rainey curled a lip. 'That's the best guess of a whore, huh?'

Her eyes flashed. 'I attended business college before I changed – professions, Todd! Why d'you think I'm here? For the adventure? I came to check the records so we'd know how much Handy had held here. I admit I never thought about Aimes transferring ready cash. It must've been on the train the other night. I remember there were *two* guards on the baggage car instead of the usual one.'

Santee recalled seeing the armed guards, too, and had briefly wondered about them. 'You'd best gather all the records you can, Deborah, and bring them along. If we take all their books, they won't know where they are and Handy won't be able to do anything until they sort it out with Head Office. Banks don't hand out any cash until they know where every cent is going and where it comes from. We've ham-strung Handy's plans to take over this bank for a while.'

'But we ain't rich like you promised!' Rainey gritted. He gave Santee a half-smile. 'Reckon the boys won't be votin' you as leader after this, drifter!'

'We can still do what we wanted. Let's get the books and clear out.'

'Do we need to bother with the goddamn books?' Skinner asked irritably, and it was the girl who answered him.

'Corey, Jed Handy would give his right arm to have these records. Without them he can't do a thing until the bank has duplicates and everything in place to their satisfaction. He won't even be able to run his ranch, if any cash transactions are necessary, until this is resolved.'

'Now I get it,' Skinner said. 'We've got the son of a bitch!'

Rainey frowned, but he looked thoughtful as the girl and Santee gathered the heavy leather-bound ledgers from the wrecked safe.

They didn't notice that Rainey had dropped back when they were leaving the deserted town, which now reeked of dynamite fumes. Only later, after they had crossed the bridge and Bourbon looked over his shoulder did they know. He took a swig from his almost empty bottle.

'Todd's draggin' tail,' he slurred, and the others saw Rainey spurring his mount out of town.

'Coming fast enough now,' allowed Skinner and hard on his words there were several explosions from the town itself.

The group reined down, waiting for Rainey to catch up, his face grinning from ear to ear.

'That'll square a few things!' he panted. Santee put his mount alongside, jostling the man.

'The hell've you done?'

'This is private,' Rainey snarled, looking back to where smoke and a few flames rose above some buildings in the business section. 'Some of them sons of bitches treated me like dirt before Handy ran me out! Wouldn't gimme credit. *'Cash on the barrelhead, Rainey, or no goods!'* Well, I showed 'em that Todd Rainey don't forget a hurt, no sir. Don't forgive and don't forget! Ever!'

He spurred away, forcing Santee to haul his horse aside as the man galloped out ahead.

'That won't endear us to the townsfolk,' Deborah said grimly. 'Are you going after him?'

Santee shook his head. 'It's done now.'

When Bodie went looking for Jed Handy

after the wake had started to break up – except for the Flying H hands who were making the most of the free booze – he found Jed still sitting at the window in Will's room in the dark.

He held a tintype of Will in his lap, as he snored, and there was an empty whiskey bottle on the floor beside the chair. No glass.

'Poor old bastard,' Bodie said quietly. 'This country din' make you, *you* made it – and now it's taken your family and all your plans are shot to hell.'

He lifted the old man easily, put him on Will's bed and stripped him down to underwear. There were scars there, on that hard old body, from Indian arrows and rustlers' bullets, and Bodie knew if he rolled Jed over he would see the ragged ridges on his back left by the raking claws of a grizzly, too. That grizzly was now in the big sitting-room downstairs in the form of a floor rug.

Old Jed was lucky to still be around after tangling with that bear. The animal had killed Handy's mount, and then raging and bleeding from some hunter's badly placed shot, turned on Jed.

The rancher dragged out his sixgun as the grizzly clasped him in a death hug, pinning his left arm between their bodies. The muzzle of Jed's sixgun was jammed against his forearm as he felt his back being ripped open. He knew he was going to die.

So he did the only thing he could – he fired the sixgun, shooting through his own arm, shattering the bone. But that first shot staggered the bear just enough to allow his arm to drop away and Jed emptied the colt into the heaving chest. The bear fell across his legs and he was pinned there for almost two days before they found him.

'You're a tough ol' son of a bitch,' Bodie told him, fondly, drawing a sheet up as Handy lay there in a drunken stupor. Bodie was pretty drunk himself and in danger of becoming maudlin.

After all, he owed his life to Jed Handy. Jed had found Bodie in a canyon down on the Palo Duro with six Commanche arrows in him – payment for fooling with some brave's squaw. Jed had shot all five Indians then doctored Bodie and taken him back to his wagon and eventually to the Flying H. He gave Bodie a good life, rearing him with his own boys, Jackson and Jedediah in their teens then, Will not yet weaned.

Bodie would never forget what he owed Jed Handy and he would literally lay down his life for the old rancher. Jed's enemies were Bodie's enemies, never mind the why or wherefore.

Wearily, he dropped into the chair by the window and looked out at the stars, breathing deeply of the night air.

The cowboys were still singing but there were not so many voices joining in now. Bodie grinned: they would all be nursing hell-bitch hangovers come morning, himself included.

He rested his head on his forearms and as he closed his eyes he heard a distant rumble of thunder. Then just as sleep caught up with him, he wondered why there was thunder when the night sky was so clear and full of stars?

But he was too tired to carry the thought through.

Which was too bad, because if he hadn't been so drunk and had taken the trouble to ride out to the north-east pasture at the foot of the Chevrons, he would have seen that the origin of the 'thunder' was the big dam Jed Handy had built between the hills so that his vast herds would have water and green grass all through the blistering Red River summers.

The dam had burst, not because of any

weakness in the high log walls or the iron-bound headgates, but because Todd Rainey planted his last seven sticks of dynamite at strategic points, cut his fuses carefully so they would burn at the same rate and explode the dynamite sticks simultaneously.

He watched it all from far up the slope above the man-made lake. The explosion sounded like a gigantic thunderclap. And then the logs split and the headgates flew wild and high into the air, as the massive wall of water that had been held back until that moment, burst forth as if it would flood the world.

It carried half the hillside away with its raging force, uprooting huge trees and boulders, surging and hammering and frothing in a muddy, seething flood as it swept down into the pastures where the Flying H herds were sleeping.

The steers leapt to their feet, bawling at a terror they could not yet see but could hear and sense.

They lunged in an instinctive stampede but the canyon mouth had been barred with a heavy log fence, rigged by Jed's cowhands so the herd would be safe while the men attended Will's funeral.

The wall of water smashed its destructive

way across the pasture, picking up cattle by the dozens, flinging them against the walls and the heavy logs – which eventually gave way, but by then the animals were drowned or so badly smashed up that they could not survive.

'*That* ought to show that goddamn 'breed and the others just who *is* fit to be leader!' Todd told himself with satisfaction; his heart was hammering against his ribs with excitement.

His horse was restless, frightened by all the noise of the rampaging water and splintering trees and the terrified bawling of the drowning cattle. Impatiently, Rainey wrenched the reins, preparing to leave – but the horse pranced and tossed its head in protest and the undermined ledge suddenly gave way. Todd Rainey cried aloud in shock as he and the poor animal hurtled down towards the chocolate-coloured, seething sea below.

10
Jed's Fury

When they got back to the hidden canyon in the late afternoon of the day of Will's funeral, Santee expected Todd Rainey to be waiting for them.

But he wasn't there. His horse, streaked with drying lather from the hard ride out from Beaumont Flats was in the corrals, still with the reins and bridle in place. The saddle had been removed but the sweat-damp blanket lay in a crumpled heap on the ground. Rainey's saddle was draped over the top rail and a spare saddle was missing.

'Where would he be?' Deborah asked them. Windy merely crowed and flapped his arms. Bourbon shrugged, uninterested. Corey Skinner, his wizened face a bit grim, said,

'Here he comes now.'

They turned to look in the direction that Skinner was pointing and saw the rider making his way down a steep trail from the rear of the canyon.

'Is there another way out of here?' Santee asked, frowning.

'Rainey says so,' Corey replied. 'Won't tell no one else where it is, though.'

Todd Rainey waved and rode up slowly. There was fresh earth on his boots and work gloves, visible when he folded his hands on the saddle-horn. He did not dismount.

'You took your time.'

'What was your hurry?' Santee asked.

'Don't like town much,' Rainey said shortly. He glanced at the sky. 'I've eaten. Oughta be a guard in case someone picks up our trail and comes in here. I'll take first watch till midnight, then Windy can relieve me.'

Windy grinned and nodded and Santee agreed. He wasn't satisfied with Rainey's behaviour – something wasn't quite right – but he said no more and Rainey flicked a two-finger salute from his hat brim, turned and rode towards the high ridge they used for look-out above the canyon's hidden entrance.

The others watched him go then dismounted and tended to their horses, Windy also rubbing down Rainey's tuckered-out mount and taking off the bridle.

In the cabin, Deborah had started to cook

a meal when Corey Skinner said, 'The son of a bitch! I mean Rainey! He had the sack with the money from the safe when we left town, but it ain't here. Just the ones with the bank ledgers in...'

Remembering the fresh earth clinging to Rainey's boots, Santee said, 'I think he buried it.'

'For safe keeping?' Deborah asked, arching her eyebrows cynically.

'I'll damn well find out when he comes back to relieve Windy!' growled Skinner. 'Windy, you wake me when Todd comes back and before you relieve, OK? You – wake – me!'

'I gotcha, Corey, I gotcha,' Windy said.

After supper, Deborah began looking through the books and soon singled out the special ledger kept for Flying H transactions. She started to explain them but Santee couldn't grasp it, Bourbon wasn't interested, Windy had already turned in and Corey Skinner merely scowled.

'We'll take a closer look in the morning,' the girl said, closing the register. 'I think we can all do with an early night. We're all tired from our adventures.'

That was one way of looking at it, thought Santee, but agreed it was a good idea for them to turn in early.

'Now don't you forget to wake me, Windy!' Skinner said, settling down.

But Windy was already snoring.

In the morning, Windy was still snoring in his bunk and Santee, first to waken, felt a lurch in his belly. There was no sign of Todd Rainey.

He shook Windy awake and asked him if Rainey had wakened him to relieve him on guard duty. But Windy had slept straight through and swore Rainey hadn't been near him.

They were all awake now and Skinner said grimly, 'I knew you couldn't trust that son of a bitch! He's vamoosed with the money!'

He was wrong.

Todd Rainey was barely alive at that moment, half-drowned, battered by flood debris, his upper body resting on a muddy slope while his legs still trailed in the sluggish waters released from the Flying H's dam by his dynamite.

The broken carcass of his horse lay in some shallows, legs in the air.

As the early sun slowly warmed him, Rainey moaned, rolled his head, but did not open his eyes. Not even when he dimly heard voices and the approaching sounds of riders making their way warily down the slippery slope towards him.

The damned hangover was bad enough, thought Jed Handy, but to wake up to the kind of news Steve Bodie had met him with was a real kick in the teeth.

'*How* many cows you say are drowned?' he demanded, immediately squinting and rubbing his wrinkled forehead hard with his hand.

'All but about fifty from the main herd in the north-east pasture, Jed,' the foreman told him quietly. His voice was rough with the aftermath of too much tobacco and booze and his face still plainly bore the marks of his fight with Wes Santee. He winced as Handy roared a curse and threw up his arms.

'Hell almighty! The cream of the crop! Judas priest, Steve, what the hell were you thinkin' about not leavin' a guard on the dam?'

'Christ, Jed, don't do that to me! You know you told me to bring in every man-jack on the payroll! Hell, this was none of my doin'. I'm just the poor stupid idiot has to give you the bad news!'

'Well, you done that, all right!' the rancher growled, his face twisted half in the pain of his hangover and half in fury at what had happened. 'Who the hell done it?'

'Dunno yet. I've got the boys searchin' them foothills. If he left any tracks we'll find 'em – and we'll find him, too, and cut his balls off!'

'You bring him to me ... whoever he is!'

'Think it was Santee?'

'More'n likely. I sent them wires for him to be intercepted but he wasn't on that train. So I figure he stayed around town and while we had everyone at Will's funeral, he...' He stopped and punched a fist into the palm of his other hand. 'Shit! That son of a bitch has set me back a whole blamed season, mebbe years.'

There was activity out in the yard and both Jed and the ramrod braved the brightness of day to go stand on the porch and see what was happening.

There was a visitor – in a surrey. Bodie shaded his reddened eyes and said, 'Damn! If that ain't Banker Aimes! The hell is *he* doin' out here so early?'

The fat banker rarely left town for any reason.

'What's he doin' out here at *all?*' de-

154

manded Jed Handy. His eyes narrowed as he noticed how reluctantly the overfed banker moved, removing his hat and turning it between his hands as he approached the porch. 'Goddammit! He ain't bringin' any good news!'

And Jed was right. Haltingly, Banker Aimes told of the blasting of his safe and the robbery, adding quickly, in a vain attempt to slightly divert the rancher's anger:

'And whoever it was blew out the back of Tracey's store, blasted part of the livery and the likker room of Bink Daniels' saloon. There were fires started, too. Lucky the town didn't burn.'

'The hell with the town!' Handy howled. 'Where's my money?'

'Oh, your money's safe, Jed,' Aimes told him with a touch more happiness. 'We transferred it to Head Office a couple of days ago, but...'

'But – *what?*'

'Well, they stole *some* money, about five thousand, all we had in the safe. And they took all the ledgers and records.'

Handy frowned. 'The hell would they do that for?'

'They can find out how much money anyone had on deposit, if they know a little about bookkeeping,' the once-again miserable banker said. 'It means, Jed, it means, no one can get any money from the bank until duplicate records are checked and authorized copies forwarded to my branch. Could take a couple of weeks – maybe longer, if I get called up there to explain...'

Jed Handy was a little slow because of his hangover, but he saw quickly enough how he had been hamstrung so that he couldn't operate the Flying H – or only to the extent of whatever cash he had on hand. Which was no more than a few hundred dollars; he never kept large sums of money around.

Banker Aimes was leaning one hand on the rail, fingers splayed, his lips pulled back tightly against his teeth, eyes wide in their sockets as he stared at Handy's darkening face. Then Jed made a growling, animal-like sound deep in his throat. He snatched Bodie's sixgun from the man's holster, and smashed the butt down on the banker's thick fingers. Aimes howled, staggered, clutching his mangled hand against him, face white and streaked with grey as the pain hit him. He looked fearfully at Jed and fell to one knee.

Handy tossed Bodie's gun back to him. 'Get him outta my sight before I kill the son

156

of a bitch!'

Bodie signed to a couple of the heavily hung-over cowhands. 'Take him to Cookie, let him bathe his hand and bandage it, then put him in his surrey and send him on his way.'

As the moaning banker was led away, Bodie shaded his eyes again. A small group of riders was coming up from the creek pasture. 'Looks like someone's hurt, Jed.'

Handy barely grunted. He didn't even look up – there was too much surging through his mind.

'Get me a hair of the dog, Steve. No, better make that the whole damn dog!'

Bodie was just going into the ranch house when he paused and looked again at the riders. 'Christ, Jed! They're bringin' in Todd Rainey!'

Handy snapped his head up this time, ignoring the pain as his brain slopped around in his skull.

'Found him half drowned near his dead hoss at the edge of the flood, boss,' a cowboy named Fuzzy McBain reported. 'There was detonators and fuse in the dead bronc's saddle-bags. This is the bastard blew our dam, all right.'

They let Rainey slide off the horse he had

been draped over and the breath whooshed out of him as he hit the hard ground of the ranch yard. Bodie stepped down and kicked him brutally in the ribs, twice. As he moaned and rolled over on his back, the ramrod yanked him half to his feet by his sodden shirt-front and flung him brutally across the steps leading up to the porch. Half conscious, Rainey lifted his out-of-focus gaze as Jed Handy drew back his boot and kicked him under the jaw.

His body hurtled backwards and he rolled down the steps on to his face in the dirt. Bodie stomped on Rainey's spine, rapped his head hard against the splintered edge of the lower step. Todd Rainey cried out as slivers of wood pierced his eyebrow and one dug deep into the bridge of his swollen nose.

Bodie heaved him up on to the porch and Jed Handy put his boot across the man's throat. He leaned down, breathing hard. 'Knew I should've killed you instead of just runnin' you off that quarter-section! You been a thorn in my side for years, Rainey, but you went too far this time! I'm all through with you. Boys, get a rope and string him up to that cottonwood. *Now!*'

McBain uncoiled his lariat and the other

two cowpokes grabbed Rainey's arms and held him. The man started to struggle but they were too strong, and in foul moods because of their thudding heads and rotgut-soured bellies. Rope lashed his wrists together and he emptied his bladder involuntarily as the noose settled over his head and was yanked tight about his throat by Steve Bodie.

Bodie jerked his head and they started to drag Rainey towards the cottonwood. The man managed to get in a lungful of air and screamed.

'*Don't!* I never did it! It – it was – Windy!' He shouted the first name that came into his head. 'Yeah, that's right, loco ol' Windy, the village idiot! He done it! Took the dynamite we brought from town and I got here too late to stop him. Honest, Jed. I ain't crazy enough to blow your dam, for Chrissakes!'

Handy glared and hit Rainey in the mouth. 'Hang the bastard anyway!'

Rainey's legs wouldn't hold him up and they half dragged, half carried him towards the cottonwood. When they started to throw the rope over a branch, he turned a white face towards Handy's uncompromising grimness.

'Jed! They took your bank records, you know!'

Handy stiffened, started forward, signing to the men to stop tossing the rope. He thrust his face close to Rainey. 'What the hell d'you know about my bank records?'

He blinked as Todd Rainey actually grinned.

'I know where they are – and I can take you to 'em. How's that? Enough to get this damn lynch-rope taken off me?'

'You don't need to *take* us anywhere!' snapped Bodie. 'We can make you tell us where the records are.'

Rainey shook his head, restraining a shudder as he felt the coarseness of the grass rope against his throat. 'You'll never find the place and, even if you did, you wouldn't find the way in. No, you need me, Jed! You want them record books, you gotta turn me loose! We got a deal?'

11
Betrayal

Todd Rainey hadn't left any tracks worth a damn.

When he had quit the hidden canyon during the night he had done so like a ghost. He wasn't heard or seen, and there was no trace of his passing.

'Always was good at coverin' his tracks,' allowed Bourbon, and the others took note of what he said because he had worked with Rainey on the latter's spread. 'We used to toss a wide-loop over some of Jed's cows if they come across the river to Todd's land and he made sure Jed never could track 'em. I reckon he stashed the money someplace and picked it up last night and vamoosed.'

Corey Skinner agreed. Windy had nothing much to say except that he had been hoping to get a few dollars so he could buy a harmonica and a 'juice' harp.

'The hell for?' growled Skinner. 'You can't play 'em.'

'I can, too! Bourbon. You've heard me

play, ain't you?'

'Well, I've heard the racket you make when you *tried* to play,' admitted Bourbon who was growing a little edgy now he had run out of booze. 'Thought someone'd stood on the cat's tail. You ask me, we're lucky you ain't got money to buy a harmonica or a Jew's harp.'

Windy pulled a face and gave a prolonged cock-crow until Skinner jostled him roughly. 'Shut up, you damn fool!'

'We oughta look around and make sure Rainey did take that money,' Bourbon said. 'He mighta been plannin' on comin' back for it later.'

'Well, why'd he run off?' Skinner demanded but Bourbon had no answer.

'I'd like to find that other way out of the canyon,' Santee said quietly. 'Rainey might not have left by the main entrance. Could be he took off out of that other exit he never told anyone about. And that's why we never found any tracks at the front.'

'Do we need to go after him?' Deborah asked. As they looked at her, she said, 'Well, I know five thousand is a lot of money but he knows this country well and he's got such a long start...'

'We risked our necks for that cash!' Skin-

162

ner said stubbornly. 'We're entitled to share it!'

Deborah studied him levelly. 'It really belongs to the townsfolk, Corey. It's Jed Handy we want to bring down.'

'Well, townsfolk never done much for me!'

Santee could see this argument going back and forth and getting nowhere. He stood abruptly. 'I'm going to take a look around and see if I can find another way out. Could be good to know about it if Handy should find this place – and he'll be looking for us once he knows the bank records have been taken.'

'Well, *I'm* gonna look for the cash,' Skinner said. 'It's just possible he might've only stashed it and aimed to come back for it later.'

Deborah said she would go with Santee and while the others pattered about, arguing amongst themselves over the most likely place for Rainey to have cached the money, the drifter and the girl rode towards the rear end of the canyon.

'I think I might be able to find the exit, Wes.'

Santee hipped in the saddle sharply. 'You know this place that well?'

She gave him a half-smile. 'When I was

here before, Todd took me with him one day when he wanted to get away from the others for a time – the other girl kept them busy, anyway. He took me into a narrow chasm-like place and showed me where a spring was bubbling up out of the ground at the base of one wall. When the sun was directly overhead it reflected off the water and threw all these marvellous patterns on the rocks. They're mostly red but there are some white and yellow and blue-grey, too, and it was quite a show – like a rainbow flickering on and off. In fact, he said it was called Rainbow Gap, but was too narrow for riders to go much past the spring.'

'You didn't think it was?' Santee prompted.

She shook her head. 'I think a rider could get through but when I said so Todd got quite irritated and only brightened up after we'd left the place and started back to the main camp.'

Santee agreed it was worth a try but Deborah couldn't find the way to the chasm, making several attempts, each time literally coming to a dead end.

They decided to rest the horses, for this was rugged country and they were wearying. They chose the shade of a tree growing amongst some boulders and Deborah took some biscuits she had fried up in the remains of the breakfast grease which she took from her saddle-bag.

'You bring that bank ledger with you?' Santee asked, frowning a little, as he caught a glimpse of the corner of a leather-bound protruding from the saddle-bag. He bit into a biscuit although it was cold it tasted fine, flavoured by bacon and the bean sauce.

'Yes. I left the other bank records but I thought Handy's book was too valuable to leave lying around. If ever we have to confront him, it could be a good bargaining piece.'

Santee smiled. 'You ain't just a pretty face, are you?' he laughed.

'Why thank you, Wes.' She paused. 'It – doesn't seem to bother you that I'm a whore.'

He shrugged. 'I've known some good whores and some bad ones, same as I've known good women and bad women. Good lawmen and bad–'

'In other words, you take folk as you find them? Never mind what they – are?'

'Like you said. As I find 'em.'

She smiled. *She knew he was her kind of man!*

Then they heard the gunfire crackling

down the canyon, coming from the main camp.

Bourbon was the first to die.

Steve Bodie led in Jed's posse, the rancher himself in the middle of the ten riders. Most of the Flying H's men were trying to salvage what they could back at the ranch. Bodie wore Abe Kirby's sheriff's star so as to give the vigilantes a semblance of legality, but it would fool no one.

Not that he cared two cents worth of goat's dung. Todd Rainey had kept his word and led them to the hideout. He was now riding alongside Handy – reluctantly, but unable to do anything about it. All the Flying H riders had their orders: if Rainey made a break for it, shoot him out of the saddle.

Jed was considering whether to shoot the son of a bitch anyway, for he hated traitors worse than liars, but he figured he would get this chore over with first and then he would decide Rainey's fate.

Bourbon was looking for the loot they were sure Rainey had buried near some rocks above a bend of the creek where Rainey used to go fishing. He figured it might be a place the man would choose to stash the stolen money. So far he had had no luck. He straightened his back with a grunt and walked stiffly to the creek, knelt down and scooped water up over his face, then slaked his thirst.

The sloshing of the water covered the sounds of the Flying H avengers coming in across the grassy flats at first, but when he squeezed the water out of his eyes he almost fell over at the sight of the big band of armed men. He made a dash for his horse, saddled and contentedly grazing by the rocks, unshipped his sixgun and fired on the run.

His bullets were wild but the men scattered and his belly flipped when he recognized Steve Bodie out in front. The man had a rifle to his shoulder and Bourbon, out of condition, breathing heavily, flung himself at his horse with a yell. It startled the mount and it shied so that he missed the reins and fell, rolling, thrusting desperately to his feet as the horse veered well out of range.

Bodie's rifle cracked, the lever blurred in its up-and-down movements, and before the first slug had struck Bourbon, the second was on its way. The double impact of the lead spun the outlaw violently. He somersaulted when he was slammed back, landed face down and barely moved, just one leg twitching. But to make sure, Steve shot him again between the shoulder blades.

Bourbon's horse ran off, but no one was interested as it raced away up-canyon. They swept past the rocks and Bourbon's body. Then they saw Corey Skinner, afoot beside his mount, unlimbering his rifle from the saddle scabbard near the top of the slope. He had been searching his own special area for the bank money when he had heard the shooting that had taken Bourbon's life. Now he had been seen and several men fired at once as he dived headlong into shelter. Bullets ricocheted with wasp-like snarls, rock dust spurting. When Corey fired back, he had crawled several feet along from the point where he had dived out of sight. He rose to one knee and his rifle worked and blasted. Two men rolled out of their saddles and a horse was shot from under a third.

Todd Rainey ducked wildly over his own mount's neck as Skinner's lead fanned his cheek. 'You goddamn yaller-belly, Rainey! We shoulda hogtied you and strung you up!'

Rainey fell out of the saddle and his shoulder was clipped by one hoof of Jed's horse. He rolled, dazed, and Handy leaned down and clubbed him with his sixgun butt, spurring for cover as Skinner opened up, emptying his gun.

'Ride him down!' yelled Jed. 'Don't give him a chance to reload!'

Skinner was already running for his horse, dragging his sixgun out of leather, abandoning the rifle. He knew he wasn't going to make it and suddenly stopped running, wrenching around to face the charging Flying H cowboys. He fanned the Colt's hammer, winging a horse and one man. Then the six men lifted their guns, rifles and revolvers, and fired. Skinner's shredded body was lifted into the air. He crashed hard on to the slope, slid down a few feet, leaving a dark stain on the earth.

'Find that drifter!' snapped Bodie, his big voice bellowing. 'And bring Windy in alive!'

Windy was a long way upstream, searching a piece of the hidden canyon he reckoned Rainey might have used to bury the money. And although Skinner and Bourbon had jeered at him, he had just uncovered it when he heard the first shots that brought down Bourbon.

He snatched the canvas sack branded with the bank's name, and, crowing like a rooster, hoofed it towards the main cabin: he hadn't brought a mount, figuring he could throw off Bourbon and Skinner better if he was afoot if they tried to follow him. Now he wished he had a horse and a gun!

I thought I brought me along my hogleg! He told himself as he felt for the holstered weapon that wasn't there. Ah, well, I know this place better'n Jed Handy.

That was true. But he was afoot and they were mounted and out for blood – Jed Handy had promised two hundred dollars to the man who found Windy, whom Rainey had blamed for the dynamiting of the Flying H dam, and five hundred for whoever found or killed Santee.

So Windy didn't have much of a chance. Three Flying H cowpokes converged on him as he staggered across a small sloping section of ground, one coming in over the top, the other two from front and back. Naturally, Windy made his run to the only open place, but they merely spurred their sweating mounts and surrounded him in seconds. He crouched, panting, eyes wide and wild, suddenly crowed, and then changed it to the howling snarl of a hunting cougar. It was realistic, spooked the mounts, and while the men were fighting the horses, cursing, he tumbled down the rest of the slope, hit the bottom running.

That was when Steve Bodie thundered out of the juniper clump, leaned out of the saddle and used his coiled lariat to smash Windy across the head and face. Windy went down, dazed and bleeding, dropping his sack of money. Steve dismounted and whistled the pre-arranged signal. Handy came riding in with two of the others. Another man led a horse with a dazed and sick-looking Rainey swaying in the saddle.

Bodie stood with one boot on the back of Windy's head as he shook out his rope. He looked up at Jed who nodded.

Although Windy screamed his innocence of dynamiting the dam, he was swinging from a cottonwood with Bodie's rope cutting deeply into his throat within five minutes.

12
Against All Odds

Bourbon's sorrel was grazing on some grass when Santee and Deborah rode out of the back end of the canyon. They saw it right away and Santee looked about quickly for sign of its rider, but he saw the fresh bullet scar on the saddle even as they heard more gunfire coming from the direction of the main camp.

Bourbon's horse lifted its head and stood patiently with ears pricked as they walked their mounts up slowly. Santee reached out and untied the rifle and scabbard attaching them to his own saddle. He slid the Winchester free, checked the load and levered a shell into the breech.

The girl had lost a little colour. She watched his every movement. Their gazes locked.

'You stay back here out of sight while I go take a look.'

She shook her head. 'I don't want to be left alone. All that shooting ... frightened me.'

'I guess it doesn't mean anything good,' the drifter allowed as fresh volleys broke out. 'But if it's Handy and his men, you'll be better out of sight.'

She placed a hand on his arm. 'You – wouldn't be silly enough to take them on single-handed, would you?'

He half smiled. 'Do I look that stupid?'

He didn't wait to hear her answer, spurred his claybank away, realizing it was already tired from the long search through that rugged country trying to locate this Rainbow Gap she had told him about. He glanced back over his shoulder once and saw she had taken up the reins of Bourbon's mount and was leading it in amongst some rocks.

Then he concentrated on getting closer to that gunfire, wondering what he was going to find – knowing deep down it wasn't going to be anything good.

It wasn't, of course. He saw smoke first and knew that it came from the cabins. He saw the riders milling about when he topped a ridge – and also saw Windy's body turning slowly in the breeze at the end of Bodie's rope, dangling from the cottonwood.

Grim-faced, he rode on down but there was nothing to be done for Windy. He cut him down and laid him out at the base of the tree, then leapt into the saddle and continued down the canyon, rifle in hand.

He found Corey Skinner next, grimacing when he saw how the little man's body had been torn apart by a dozen bullets.

By that time, they had seen him.

The main camp was just over the low ridge where Corey Skinner had died. Handy had apparently left a man on look-out. He triggered three fast shots into the air to attract the attention of the others as they watched the cabins burn, then he lowered his gun to shoot at Santee. The drifter's rifle was already at his shoulder and the Flying H man was punched back over his horse's rump, spilling untidily to the ground. Then Jed Handy and Steve Bodie came sweeping over the crest, followed by half a dozen cowboys. Santee was surprised to see Todd Rainey riding with them, although the man didn't have a gun and seemed to be herded along by others.

He knew right away how Handy and his men had found the hideout and he paused even as lead burned the air about him. The rifle was rock steady and Santee seemed immune to the bullets that were coming his way. He didn't flinch, concentrated his shot on Rainey.

The outlaw saw he was the target, knew as plainly as if Santee had shouted it out. He gave a whining cry, wrenched his mount aside, crashing into another rider, trying to get out of the crush of men and horses.

He managed it – helped by Santee's bullet.

It took Rainey smack in the middle of the chest and he was slammed sideways. He fell down between the horses and four of them trampled his body, the mounts shying and whinnying as they felt his flesh underfoot.

Santee was spurring away and felt the burn of a bullet across his back as he hunched over the claybank's arched neck, rifle held out to one side. Handy and Bodie led the shouting men down the slope after him. Santee suddenly reared up straight in the saddle, bringing up the Winchester, raking the ragged line with his fire.

A hat flew into the air. A horse plunged and reared, throwing its rider. A man jerked and sobbed in pain as a slug took him in the shoulder, wrenching him sideways in the saddle. The man alongside reached out and pushed him back onto his horse, but he was swinging the mount away from the others, already sick with pain, arm dangling use-lessly.

The rifle-hammer fell on an empty breech and Santee sheathed the gun, raked with the spurs and flicked the reins, urging the claybank to lengthen its stride. It sounded like a full-scale battle and, briefly, Santee found himself listening for Indian war cries or the clash of cavalry sabres. This was brought about by the narrowing canyon walls flinging the intermingling echoes back and forth.

Then the claybank broke stride, and he heard its whinnying snort, felt and saw the head and mane jerk wildly. The horse was already going down as he snatched the rifle from the saddle scabbard, threw a leg over the horn and dived into a clump of chaparral. It broke his fall but it was brittle dry and breaking twigs scratched at his face, just missing his eyes, tore red gashes across the backs of his hands, ripped his shirt.

But he rolled away from the place he had entered and squirmed beneath the brush, lying on his side, panting, as he shucked cartridges from his bullet belt and thumbed them home into the rifle's breech. The Flying H crew reined down, forming a ragged line beyond the edge of the chaparral.

'Come out or burn, 'breed!' bellowed Steve Bodie. 'They're the only choices you got!'

'We mean it, Santee!' called Jed Handy. 'You're gonna die anyway, but *how* you die could turn out to be mighty important to you!'

'You got another rope?' Santee yelled and fired even as he spoke, aiming for Handy through the screening brush. But while the Winchester slug is devastating in its effect, it is essentially slow-moving and even its bulk can be deflected by what might seem to be an insignificant twig.

Which is what happened – and the bullet flew wide. But his voice had given them a target and they poured a volley into the chaparral, leaves and dust and grit and stones kicking into Santee's face as he frantically rolled away from his position.

There were three or four desultory, searching shots and then Handy said, 'That fool Windy blew down my dam – as if you didn't know! He deserved to swing!'

Santee cursed Todd Rainey. So that was where he'd been last night! Dynamiting the Flying H dam and when he was caught, he put the blame on poor Windy – and to save his own neck, led Handy's men in here...

He hoped Rainey was dying hard, coughing out his life, alone and in the dust on top of that ridge.

Then he smelled the smoke.

And heard the crackling of flames.

Through the sudden roaring sound, he heard Steve Bodie's deep bellow: 'What's left of you ain't gonna be buried, 'breed! We're leavin' it for the coyotes and vultures!'

Santee had no doubt that that was just the kind of miserable gesture Bodie was capable of but he was already moving backwards and to one side. The fire was raging through the tinder-dry chaparral and rapidly overtaking him. The only way he stood a chance of out-distancing it, was to get up on his feet and *run*.

And he would make a perfect target for the waiting range-men if he did.

Forcing down the urge to leap up, he scrambled as fast as he could on hands and knees, trying to remember how large the patch of brush was and where its edges finished. Some just petered out into weeds and short grass, one at least ended up near the rocks where the back part of the canyon began. If he could make it to there he might stand a chance. Deborah was somewhere in that vicinity and she had taken Bourbon's horse with her...

He had to try. Already his eyes were watering and the tears were half-blinding him.

His throat was burning like acid from the smoke. The heat was beating at his body like a live thing, wrapping about him, scorching his exposed flesh, causing the ragged tears in his clothes to smoulder. Hell, this kept up and there wouldn't be enough left of him to give the buzzards a decent feed!

The thought somehow dragged up reserves of energy and he tugged his neckerchief tightly around the lower part of his face, pulled the brim of his hat low, and scrambled in the direction he hoped would lead him to the rocky area. By now the smoke was so thick he couldn't get any direction and he was disorientated from trying to find a way around the fire; it was closing in on him from many directions and he guessed men had started several fires in different locations.

It was mighty hard to breathe. He swore there was an iron band being screwed up tighter with every move about his chest. The world had disappeared. There was nothing left but swirling smoke, leaping tongues of flame licking at him, and unburned brush snagging his clothes, holding him as if it wanted him to be consumed along with itself when the flames reached this spot.

He tore free, weaker than he thought, head

spinning, ears roaring with the thunder of the fire, choking on the smoke, his movements slowed now. His hand touched the rifle barrel and it was *hot,* searing his flesh. He quickly changed his grip to the wooden stock, not yet ready to abandon all hope. A dagger of fire licked his left ear and he shouted aloud in pain as the hair on his temple singed and shrivelled. Rubbing a quick handful of dust against his face, he lunged away, even the soles of his boots were hot to the touch now.

It was no use. He didn't know where he was, which way to turn. He couldn't breathe. His knees were raw and bleeding as were the palms of his hands. He was almost blinded by the smoke and his brain reeled from lack of oxygen.

Well, he had drifted for years since he had lost his family, uncaring whether he lived or died – and now he was going to die.

And suddenly he realized that he did care whether he lived or died. *And he was thinking of Deborah…*

'Wes! Wes!'

He blinked. Through the roaring in his head he heard her voice. And figured he must be close to dying … but then he *did* hear her – again. Calling his name. *Left!*

181

Over to the left! his reeling mind told him. He paused briefly to work out which side was left and then lunged that way, making choking sounds as the effort called for more oxygen than his aching lungs could supply.

But he felt something slap across his shoulders, slither down the side of his singed face and immediately his brain screamed *snake!* But it wasn't a snake: he put down his hand and felt the rough twist of a rope beneath his raw palm. His fingers closed around it and he pushed the rifle through his belt at his back, took the rope in both hands and tugged to let her know he had a hold of it.

He was literally torn from the fire, bursting through it in a surging, crashing, searing rush and only afterwards did he figure out she had her end of the rope tied around the saddle horn, using her horse to pull him free. He let go and rolled away, coming up against rock, breath gushing from him. He lay there gagging on the fresh air, only thin tendrils of smoke coiling around him now.

Then she was pouring a canteen of water over him, soothing his burned and blistered flesh and for a few moments he didn't care if he did die – it would be worth it just for this cool cascade.

'We have to move!' She was kneeling beside him, shaking him. 'Oh, you look terrible. But we can't stay. The smoke will clear in a few minutes when the last of the chaparral burns out. Can you ride?'

'Get me – on my – feet!' he croaked. She helped him up, and they limped and staggered together towards the waiting horses.

'I found the way into Rainbow Gap,' she told him. 'It was hidden by brush and Bourbon's horse plunged when a snake rattled and broke the bush down...'

'Told you – you weren't just – a – a pretty face!' he gasped and didn't remember the next few minutes until much later.

'The *hell* could he've gotten outta that fire!' demanded Jed Handy, his heart hammering as the rage took control. 'Have another look through the ashes!'

'Judas, Jed, a blind man could see there's nothin' there!' complained Bodie. His eyes were reddened by smoke and his lungs felt seared. For many years, tough as he was, he had been plagued by bronchitis, especially in the winter, but smoke was always an irritant. And he felt as if that damn chaparral fire was still burning – inside his chest. It was making him mighty cantankerous. A deep cough racked him.

Handy merely stared hard at him and the ramrod sighed, waved a hand to the other blackened cowboys.

'Search the ashes *again*, boys.'

They obeyed, knew better than to complain, although it was obvious Santee had escaped.

'There's some burned rope here!' called Charley Cain and they all gathered around quickly, handling the pieces of charred rope.

After that it wasn't hard to read the scuff signs where Santee had been dragged clear.

'He's got someone helping him!' Handy said. 'Now who the hell...?'

Steve Bodie, too impatient to enter into conjecture, was down on one knee examining the tracks. 'Two horses. One's Bourbon's but I don't recognize the other tracks.' He stood and pointed into the rapidly narrowing canyon. 'In there...'

'That don't lead nowhere,' Jed growled. 'Look how narrow it gets. Rider would only jam himself up in there.'

'There could be another way out,' Steve said thoughtfully. 'Todd Rainey wasn't the kind who'd hide out without havin' a bolt hole or an extra escape route.'

'Get lookin' then!' snapped Jed, wearying

of this chase now. He absently massaged his aching left shoulder.

Charley Cain led the way in and the men rode with guns out, shaking their heads, sure it was a waste of time. Bodie paused and looked up at the towering walls: they seemed to be toppling inwards and he flinched: claustrophobia was something else that had long troubled him and he was not comfortable down here. He looked for a way to climb out...

Jed brought up the rear, mouth tight with the anger simmering within him. 'Keep going!' he snapped.

The girl found the brush-choked entrance to Rainbow Gap and immediately Santee felt the crushing effect of the high, narrow walls, like some great knife-slash in the rocks.

The walls towered sixty or seventy feet above them, fairly smooth, but with some projections here and there that made it apparently impossible for a rider to get by. They dismounted and Santee sent the girl ahead while he led the horses, one behind the other, using the remains of the rope to tie them together. He held the reins of Bourbon's mount and Deborah's grey followed, more at ease than the other horse. He could hear the bubbling spring and when they rounded a tight bend, the stirrups having to be hooked over the saddle horns so as to give passage, he saw it.

A crystal clear pool with a light greenish tinge, ripples at one end rising and spreading, marking the points below the surface where the water bubbled in through a crack in the rock. It must drain from a hollow worn in the soft sandstone over the ages, he reckoned. The chasm narrowed sharply immediately beyond the pool and it was a hard job dragging the horses through. Their sides touched the rock walls, scraping against the cinch straps and flaps and saddle-bags. The girl's mount in particular seemed disturbed by the closeness of the high walls: whinnying, rolling its eyes, snorting, communicating its fear to Bourbon's sorrel. Santee cursed, the rope was hurting his raw palms as he leaned his weight back into it, pulling, digging in with his heels. The girl edged back to lend a hand but there wasn't enough room.

'Keep – going!' Santee gasped. 'I thought – I heard – riders – back there. Just a click or two like horseshoes – striking rock...'

She looked sharply past him; but there was

nothing to see but the struggling horses, and then she turned and continued on, calling, 'I can see the end! It widens gradually!'

Santee silently thanked God, or someone, for that as he heaved and swore and cajoled until finally the horses were through. Panting, sweating, he saw that the girl was right. Forty yards ahead was the vertical slash of the narrow exit, showing a slab of blue sky. The walls opened out a little, enough for the horses to walk without scraping the sides, and Santee hurried them up.

Ten minutes later, they were through Rainbow Gap, and the shadows were already darkening the narrow way as the sun tilted into the western sky. Santee was exhausted and she gave him a canteen with a little water remaining in it which he used to rinse out his mouth, swallowing only a trickle.

'Some of those burns need attention,' Deborah said, starting to dampen a cloth, but he shook his head, went to the horse and took his rifle out of the scabbard, which was all scuffed and torn in places from the rough passage through the chasm.

'Later. They're comin' after us. If I hide out in those rocks yonder, I can cover that gap and pick 'em off one by one.'

'Wes, no! We should go, get right away from here.'

'They're gonna keep coming, Deborah.'

'I – know. But...'

'I can hold out here as long as my ammo lasts.' He worked the lever on the rifle. 'You ride out, head back to Beaumont Flats or go on to the next town. You got that bank record so, if worse comes to worst...'

Suddenly she paled as she turned to her horse. 'No! It's not here! The saddle-bag's all torn, the stitching has broken from scraping against the rock I suppose ... it must've fallen out.'

Santee stifled a curse: if the book had dropped and Handy's men were coming after them, they would find it – and then there would be nothing to bargain with if it came to a showdown.

He was already on his feet, moving in a staggering lope towards the chasm. The girl called his name twice, urgently, but he kept going without looking back, rifle held in front of him.

It was easier squeezing through without having to drag the horses, too, and he was soon back at the pool, panting, sweating, eyes scanning every inch of the ground for the ledger. He couldn't see it and he was certain that this was the area where it must have been lost, for he had seen it sticking out of the saddle-bag when he had looped the stirrups up over the saddle horns.

He knelt by the pool, scooped water over his hot face with its blisters; some layers of skin flaked away. He swallowed a little. It was strongly mineral and rasped his throat and – *there was the ledger!*

It was lying on the bottom of the pool. He lay down, hearing again the clicking of horseshoes back there and echoing along the chasm as Handy and his men searched for a way through. The narrow walls acted as an amplifier. He couldn't quite reach the book, took a breath and immersed his head and shoulders, the greenish water stinging his eyes and yet feeling good at the same time after the smoke. His fingers touched the cover. He strained a little more, hooked his fingers underneath and stood the book on end. Before it could topple again, he grasped it and surged back, gasping, pulling the book with him.

Then a gun roared like a cannon in the confined space of Rainbow Gap and there were several snarling buzz-like sounds as the bullet ricocheted from wall to wall, kicking rock chips and dust down into the pool.

Santee rolled away, rifle in one hand, dripping ledger in the other. He glimpsed a man back there levelling a rifle and once again the shot slammed from wall to wall, zigzagging through and whining away. He turned, dropped the book, and triggered three fast shots into the gap. A man screamed in pain, for it was narrower back there and he had no way of retreating with others pushing from behind. His body fell and jammed the way, at least temporarily.

Santee scooped up the book and ran back the way he had come, moving more confidently now, trying to ignore the pain of his burns and the aching muscles of his abused body.

The girl was mounted just beyond the exit, holding the reins of the other horse ready for him. He tossed her the dripping ledger and she put it in the good saddle-bags as he clambered into saddle.

'Ride! Ride!' he gritted, slapped his scorched hat against her horse's rump. She gave a small cry as it jumped away and broke into a run immediately, glad to get away from this claustrophobic area.

Santee spurred after her, intending to wheel into the bounder clump and start shooting into the chasm. But there was an unexpected shot from above and the horse lurched and whinnied as the bullet gouged its shoulder, causing it to break stride. He fought the reins, almost dropping his rifle and the gun above fired again, lead kicking stones and grit just in front of the stumbling horse.

'Haul rein, 'breed!' bellowed Steve Bodie from the top of the cliff, rifle at his shoulder again. 'Do it or I shoot the gal!'

Deborah had instinctively slowed when the gun had first fired and she wheeled her horse, watching as Santee fought to hold his mount upright. But its right foreleg crumpled and he spilled from the saddle. He still retained his hold on the rifle, and came up to his knees but Bodie put a bullet into the ground in front of him.

He dropped the rifle and lifted his hands shoulder high.

'Now the sixgun!' Bodie ordered and Santee obeyed. 'Woman, you climb on down and just stand there. You move and I'll shoot Santee in the leg. *He* tries anythin' and I'll shoot *you* in the leg! OK. Just stay like that – Jed and the boys'll be along right soon.'

'Oh, my God, Wes! What're we going to do now!' Deborah gasped, edging closer to him.

'We've still got the book to bargain with.'

He heard her suck down a sharp breath. He snapped his head around. She shook her head briefly. 'It opened as I was stowing it in the saddle-bag. The water, or the minerals in it, has made the ink run. You can't read a thing! It's just a meaningless blob!'

13
One Man Riot

Bodie must have grown impatient waiting for Jed Handy and the others to make their way through the chasm. He called out to Santee and the girl to lie flat on their faces with their arms spread like a pair of crucifixes.

Then he began to climb down from the cliff, picking a steep trail that had likely been used by mountain goats or bighorn sheep. He slipped a couple of times and although Santee lifted his head hopefully, Bodie was slick and had the rifle covering him in an instant.

Panting, coughing once or twice and grasping at his aching chest, the ramrod walked across and kicked Santee in the side.

'Sit up and keep your hands where I can see 'em.' He leaned down and flipped Santee's hunting knife from its sheath, tossing the weapon to one side. He spoke to Deborah roughly. 'You can sit up, too, whore! Any smart moves and I'll shoot the 'breed – not to kill, just to bust him up a little.'

Deborah, pale and strained-looking, got to her knees and although Bodie snapped he hadn't told her to stand, she stood anyway and brushed down her clothes.

'Let her go, Bodie,' Santee said. 'We can give you Jed's bank records. She's nothing to do with this, just got caught up in it. She's no threat to you.'

Bodie kicked Santee. 'Shut up, 'breed! Jed's gonna decide what happens.' He grinned tightly. *'I* know he's gonna gimme you and that's all I want.'

'First licking you've ever had?' asked Santee, rubbing it in and it earned him another kick.

Bodie glanced towards the chasm where they could hear the others now and said, 'More to it than that. Will was a brat, but he was Jed's brat. And you killed him, Santee. You're a dead man already, just don't know it yet.'

And then Jed Handy led four bedraggled cowboys out of the chasm, their horses trailing them. Handy looked near exhaustion but he brightened when he found Santee and the girl were prisoners.

'Was worth your while makin' that climb

over the top, after all, Steve. So, you had a whore to help you, drifter! You shoulda kept your nose outta this, Dorm or whatever your name is. Now you gotta die, too.'

Deborah sat down suddenly, her legs apparently unable to support her at this news. Handy curled a lip and set his gaze on Santee.

'Was just telling Bodie, we have the bank ledger, Handy. She just got caught up in this. She can't harm you. Take the book and turn her loose. What good can it do you killing her?'

Jed Handy leaned down towards Santee, his eyes narrowed. 'She slapped Will's face once! He tended to get a mite rough with his women and she slapped him! A god-damn *whore*, slappin' my boy! Ah, no, Santee, she's in this whether she likes it or not.'

'You're a miserable sonuver, Jed!' the drifter said but Handy didn't rise to the bait.

He merely grinned tightly and then kicked Santee in the thigh which showed red and raw from the fire through a rent in his trousers. The drifter grunted in pain and fell onto his side. Deborah quickly knelt beside him, looking up angrily at the rancher.

'Leave him alone! None of this is his doing! He only wanted work when he came to town!'

'It all started with him!' shouted Jed, breathing hard, passion taking his breath. 'That half-breed son of a bitch made trouble as soon as he hit town! And he started everythin'. Kirby on his side, fightin' my men, and ended up killin' my last son!' His voice cracked a little. 'An' you say *leave him alone*. I'll leave him, all right – dead an' unburied right out here where the animals can pick at what's left of him!' He was shaking with his hate and snapped at Bodie while still watching Santee. 'Gimme a knife!'

'Take it easy, Jed!' warned Bodie worriedly. 'Remember your ticker!'

'Gimme a goddamn knife!'

Jed turned sharply and staggered, suddenly looking very grey. His face twisted in pain as he clawed at his chest. Bodie grabbed at him quickly and the other men moved in as the ramrod lowered the rancher gently to the ground.

'God almighty! It's his heart,' Bodie gritted. 'All this has been too damn much for him!'

He snapped at one of the men to bring

196

water. The cowboy hurried to get a canteen from his horse and they gathered around while Bodie ripped open the old man's shirt, tilted the canteen against his purple lips.

'Come on, Jed, old feller! Come back to us!' Santee was surprised by the tenderness in the ramrod's voice.

Deborah eased closer to Santee and pressed something into his hand. He was startled, but didn't need to look down to tell what it was.

It was the four-barrelled Remington derringer she carried for protection.

'He needs a sawbones. Chick, you and Walt get him on his horse and ride with him. Rocky, you ride hell for leather to town and then ride back with the sawbones and meet up with Chick and Jed. *Move*, God-damnit, or we're gonna lose him!'

He barely glanced at Santee as he organized his men and they roped the ailing rancher in his saddle. Rocky, already on his horse, spurred away.

'There's a trail around this mesa,' Bodie called after him. 'Bear left through the trees – I seen it from on top of the cliff! And bring that sawbones out to meet Jed if you have to haul him behind you on a rope! And don't stop for nothin', none of you. *Christ, come on,* Chick! Get movin'!'

The remaining cowboy, known only as Pecos, a lean, hardfaced man with only half an ear, held his rifle on Santee while Bodie, obviously anxious, watched the others ride out with Jed, steadying the semi-conscious in the saddle.

When they had disappeared into the trees, searching for the trail he had described, he turned back to Santee and the girl. He stooped and picked up the drifter's hunting knife, testing the blade with his calloused thumb. Deborah stiffened as he walked across.

'Seems the old man favoured havin' you cut into little pieces 'breed. Well, whatever Jed wants is OK by me! We'll start with your ears and work our way down. How's that sound?'

Deborah gasped and Bodie gave her a crooked grin. 'Well, I dunno. Maybe I should start with *you*, whore! I can see Santee's taken a shine to you – ought to turn his stomach seein' you carved up, eh? Well, I'm all for anything' that'll add to his sufferin', so you look like you've run outta luck!'

Deborah started to turn to run and Bodie laughed, reaching for her – and then Pecos yelled suddenly:

'Steve! Watch the 'breed!'

He brought his rifle up as Santee rolled away from the girl. The bullet kicked a handful of gravel as he spun onto his side and brought up the Remington, bucking in his hand. The bullet took Pecos in the shoulder, shattering bone, causing the man to cry out in pain, the rifle falling. The man was game, though, and grabbed at his sixgun as Santee pushed the ring-trigger forward, thereby rotating the firing pin to the next barrel. *Pulling* the ring cocked the hammer and fired the .32 calibre cartridge into the cowboy. As the man doubled up and fell, Santee, still making his turn towards Bodie, flung himself aside – barely in time.

The ramrod's sixgun ripped out of leather but Bodie fired too early in his hurry to nail the drifter. The bullet thudded into the sand where Santee's body had been a split second before. The drifter triggered the derringer, but in his haste he hadn't lined up the firing-pin properly and it misfired. Bodie shot again and Santee felt the wind of the slug past his face as he bounced to his knees, launched himself in a headlong dive for his rifle, abandoning the derringer. He scooped up the rifle and twisted violently, back towards Bodie, causing the man to overshoot with his next two shots. And then Santee was rising to one knee, the rifle-butt braced into his hip, working trigger and lever in a blur of speed and crashing gunfire.

Bodie jerked with the strike of lead, twisted around by the second and third bullets. He dropped to his knees, blood already flecking his mouth. He sagged there, still holding his smoking sixgun, eyes rolling in his head, but by some force of will he brought them into focus and started to lift his Colt.

'Jed – said you – have to – die…' he rasped, then he pitched forward on his face, his gun going off but the bullet driving into the ground right in front of him.

Santee eased the pressure off the rifle's trigger, stood up and walked across. He got a boot under Bodie's thick shoulder and heaved him over on to his back.

The man was not yet dead. He tried one more time to shoot the drifter but the shot was mighty wild. Santee kicked the gun out of his hand.

Bodie glared up at Santee, dredging up his hatred from deep down, blood running over his chin now. 'You won't – live long – Jed'll put a – bounty on you – 'br – 'breed –You – Will – Jed won't forget – I done my – best – Jed – I…'

There was a fit of coughing that sprayed bright blood over Santee's boots and lower legs and then Steve Bodie died at last. Jed Handy's name on his lips.

Santee lowered the rifle's hammer and turned to Deborah who was shaking. He slipped his free arm about her slim waist and she pressed tightly against him for comfort, her head resting against his shoulder.

'Will the others come back?' she asked, looking anxiously at the trees.

'Don't think so. Bodie told 'em not to turn back for anything. They'll just think Bodie was having some fun, shooting us to pieces, if they heard the gunfire.'

She shuddered. 'Can we – can we get out of here, Wes?'

'Sure.'

It was a long ride back to Beaumont Flats and they took the sack containing the five thousand dollars with them.

They saw Handy's men standing outside Bink Daniels' partly burned saloon, drinks in their hands. They didn't seem to know quite what to do about Santee.

But they stiffened and changed their drinks to their left hands, keeping their gun hands free, as he dismounted and, after helping

Deborah down, walked up on to the saloon porch.

'Jed make it?' the drifter asked and after a hesitation, Chick answered.

'He made it. But he ain't too good. Doc said it was a stroke, not his ticker. He won't be able to talk or walk, and likely won't last more'n a couple months.'

'What happens about the ranch?'

Chick shrugged. 'Dunno and don't care. Me and the boys won't be around. If Jed can't run the place – or what's left of it after Rainey blowin' the dam – we ain't gonna get paid so we're movin' on.'

Santee nodded, raking all three with his soul chilling eyes.

'You better hope I don't run into you.'

They said nothing, but Chick spilled some of his beer getting it up to his mouth. When Santee turned he saw Muffy Cadell leading Deborah by the arm back towards the doors of the Dovecot.

'Looks like the valley's gonna be opened up for settlement again,' Santee said, and as Muffy turned, asked, 'Where you taking her, Muffy?'

The woman frowned. 'Where do you think?'

Santee limped up, shaking his head and

smiling at Deborah.

'No. We've got a far piece to travel. So we'll just get ourselves cleaned up, buy some new clothes and mounts and be on our way.'

Muffy arched her eyebrows and turned to the girl. 'That what you want?'

'I – I think so, Muffy.'

'Well, the town's mighty grateful for what you've done, Wes. I think they'll provide you with everything you need.' Muffy smiled at Deborah. 'You should be all right with this – drifter. If you don't know how to keep a man happy now – well, I just *can't* be that bad a teacher!'

Deborah actually blushed and later, when they were readying their fresh mounts and a packhorse provided by the town, she asked,

'Are you sure about this, Wes?'

'I am.'

'What are we going to do?'

'First, I'd sure like to meet this uncle of yours.'

Alarm showed on her face. 'You're not going to...'

'I won't kill him, but I'll sure have a talk with him about selling you like a piece of meat.'

'Wes, don't you understand that that

doesn't matter any longer? All I want is to get my father's ranch back...'

'And I'll help you do it. My way.' He grinned as he helped her mount. 'Save you some money in legal fees.'

Her eyes roved across his battered face and she smiled suddenly. 'Good. I'll put it towards a wedding dress.'

He surprised himself by not coming up with any objection to that.

The publishers hope that this book has given you enjoyable reading. Large Print Books are especially designed to be as easy to see and hold as possible. If you wish a complete list of our books please ask at your local library or write directly to:

Dales Large Print Books
Magna House, Long Preston,
Skipton, North Yorkshire.
BD23 4ND

This Large Print Book, for people
who cannot read normal print,
is published under the auspices of

THE ULVERSCROFT FOUNDATION